SPIN

GENEVIEVE RAAS

Ravenwell Press

 Published in the United States by Ravenwell Press.

Ravenwell Press Paperback ISBN: 978-1-944912-16-1
eBook ISBN: 978-1-944912-04-8

Second Edition

PROLOGUE

OR KINDLY WORDS OF WARNING TO THE PROSPECTIVE BUYER

NAMES ARE RATHER silly, aren't they?

It's just one word. One little word that defines us, distinguishing us from one another. If used properly they can instill fear or love in those we influence, creating a memory that lasts through the ages. Memories soon become stories that turn into fairy tales, allowing a taste of immortality.

But, I digress. Here I am rambling about names and forgetting to mention my own! I am your ever-devoted servant, Rumpelstiltskin.

I might be what they call a celebrity of sorts, my name reaching the ears of the farthest kingdoms. Need a wish? Just sign the dotted line and all your dreams will be fulfilled. It's a hobby of mine. I thrive on the rush of the quill scribbling in earnest over the parchment, the heart's desire overpowering the reason of the brain.

Too poor to pay? Don't fret. I don't discriminate—something Death and I both have in common—dealing with the lowliest of peasants to the highest of kings. I am eternally eager to bargain for what I feel is fair. There is always a price one is willing to pay past gold and jewels.

Besides, it is sometimes the simplest of possessions, possessions others see no value in, that are in fact the most valuable of all.

I have made five thousand three hundred and thirty-two deals through the centuries, watching humanity destroy itself one by one over the stupidest of reasons. I am still surprised by how far they are willing to go simply for a bit of lace or drink, something superficial that is enjoyed for a moment and gone the next, lost in their memories until the cycle begins again and they start to want once more. I am always there, feeding their desires, their addictions.

This has caused a fair amount of my patrons to call me cruel. But I ask you this...is it truly cruel to ensure I am only paid what we agreed upon?

But there I go again, bothering you with my own particular philosophies! Let's be honest. You aren't interested so much in what I feel as what I have accomplished.

Just like all of the deals I've ever made, I can tell you my journey came with a price...a lust for revenge that consumed me, and though it infested what little humanity remained in my heart, I relished every moment.

CHAPTER ONE

Spin:

verb: draw out (wool, cotton, or other material) and convert it into threads, either by hand or with machinery.

noun: a particular bias, interpretation, or point of view, intended to create a favorable (or sometimes, unfavorable) impression

THE FIRST DAY: RUMPELSTILTSKIN

Yes, she was quite intriguing. It seemed a pity that I had to break her.

THE FIRST DAY: LAILA

After my mother's death, I was at the complete mercy of my father. To put it plainly, he was a drunk, spending what little money our small mill earned on liquor and women instead of food for his family. Forgetting his own pain came at the cost of his child, and I often believed my mother was lucky the plague took her when it did.

Father had another vice that caused me greater fear than being turned out on the streets. He loved to boast, and my heart was crowded with humiliation and anger because of it.

I hated the jackals he attracted to our doors from this dangerous pastime. He would tell of great adventures he never took, discoveries he never made, and of his singular daughter, who possessed talents she never had. It made me ill imagining how he drank in the impressed gazes of the crowd, as his tapestry of lies grew ever thicker.

Now I was one and twenty and working as hard as any man trying to escape the threat of ruin. All I had was the prospect of a fortuitous marriage, but who would have me in this state? Not even Ernis, the fishmonger's son, wanted to make me an offer anymore.

I dragged a full sack of flour across the dirt floor and threw it with the others. The fire behind me snapped and spit, and I ducked just in time to miss the low beams of our sinking home. The walls leaned to the right, and when the wind blew the entire building moaned.

Shaking off the layer of flour from my skin, I looked back at the orders still waiting to be filled. Eight bags, each promising the coins we so desperately needed to survive. My fingers ached, but rest was a luxury I couldn't afford.

Besides, the pain distracted me from thinking of my father's ramblings at the pub. Last year, one of his tales nearly got us arrested. He claimed he killed a king's deer, and that I cooked it into a stew more delicious than the crown's own cook's. Thankfully, I was able to prove our innocence and the gallows were averted. This time.

Moments like that made my black thoughts boil and seethe, though I hated to admit to them. My life was a never-ending series of nightmares thanks to that man. Resentment festered, and in the deepest part of my heart, I secretly wished death would take him, for my sake, but also for his. Maybe then, he would finally be free from his pain.

I was just tying the sack closed when I heard footsteps approaching outside. It was early morning by now, just in time for my father to come home from the pub and sleep off the whiskey. If I were lucky, he would be too drunk to tell me of his conquests...or his lies.

Gravel and dirt crunched beneath his feet in a nerve-wracking rhythm. But as they drew closer, the sound grew into a terrifying, muffled chorus of footsteps, jangling metal, and indistinct shouts.

I dropped the sack and opened the door to see four guards marching towards our mill, a mule following behind them. The mule dragged a small prison wagon, my father its rope-bound cargo. My cheeks flushed with anger and fear.

A rough hand pushed me out of the way as the guards filled the room, the pungent smell of beer, dirt, and horses wafting around them.

"Father! What have you done?" I asked hotly as they dragged him inside, his face ashen as he blubbered nonsense about spinning wheels and gold.

I was stopped by the outstretched arm of a particularly grisly-looking guard with a mesh of scars stretching like a net across his face.

An insignia of a lion roaring on his breastplate told me he was not just a simple guard, but their captain.

"This the girl?" the captain demanded of my father, a sneer stretching the scars into a gruesome map as he turned to me. He grabbed my hands and examined them closely.

"I told them! I told them about your spinning, Laila!" Father whimpered. "But they wouldn't believe your gifts otherwise. I couldn't have them thinking I produced a talentless daughter. I had no choice but to protect my honor."

"You fool!" I cried. Horror rushed like cold water over every muscle of my body. "What have you told them this time? What lies have you spewed out of that foul mouth of yours?"

He only quivered like a common street rat and for the first time in his life was silent. I was on my own to save our lives, just as before with the deer.

"Your presence is required immediately before the king," the captain's voice cut in. "Your father finally revealed the secret you've been keeping hidden from his majesty. You're both lucky if you don't lose your heads for concealing such an extraordinary gift. If you can do half of what we heard, the king is in for quite the surprise."

"I don't have any secrets," I seethed, standing before the captain. "Whatever he has told you is a delusion. A bit of whiskey and a great deal of madness."

His eyes narrowed and he pointed a callused finger at me.

"That is for the king to decide," he hissed back. "You might be playing the fool with me, but I wouldn't try that little game with his majesty if I were you."

"I would not dare jest about something like this," I pleaded. "Don't you realize my father is out of his mind? Look at him! Look around you. Count the leaks coming in through the roof! We have nothing. Can't you see?"

"Do you really want to know what I see?" the captain snapped. "What I see are either two peasants keeping a secret and preventing the king from what he is owed, or two liars that deserve to be hanged for treason."

His breath stank of ale. Rage ate at me that he insisted on believing my drunken father's drunken lies. Fear made me bold.

"I demand you tell me what secret I am accused of keeping," I stated coldly. "What treason have I committed?"

"*She demands*," another guard mocked. Laughter erupted all around, its dark, full sound making me feel small—worse, weak and helpless. "For someone who can spin straw into gold, you'd expect she'd be a bit more refined in her manner of speaking."

The sensation of fire seared my lungs and charred my hope as everything became clear.

"Is that truly what this is all about?" I wheezed, pushing the words through my tightening throat. "You think I can spin straw into gold? Surely you know that's not possible! It's only the ravings of a drunk! Father, tell them the truth. Tell them it was only the drink!"

My father gazed glassily at me, his lips stubbornly slack. Every second of silence that followed might as well have been a knife in my back.

The captain laughed deep from his lungs as he patted my father on the shoulder.

"Good lad. For once your father knows when to keep silent," he said. "You, on the other hand, could learn a lesson from him. I have dogs that are trained better than you."

I couldn't control my temper any longer. Before I realized what foolishness I was doing my hand flew out towards his face, but his hand gripped my wrist, stilling my attack. My head snapped back as strong fingers grabbed my hair. The cold bite of a dagger pressed against my neck as the captain seethed.

"Such violence is not becoming of a woman, although it is hard to tell if you even are a woman under such a layer of filth." His men roared with laughter. "I've had enough of your theater. If you say one more word, I swear I will cut out your tongue! You don't need to talk to spin gold for the king. Follow your father's example. I told him if he remained quiet he might stand a chance of survival, and so far he is thriving."

I knew it was useless, even treasonous to fight. Yet, I couldn't help struggling against his grip as he bound my hands with rope. My legs flailed and jerked as I kicked out. I spit in their faces as I tried to pull away again, but their grips only tightened.

I struck one's face with my foot with a resounding, satisfying crack, and his nose spurted blood.

"Make her still!" he exclaimed, wiping the crimson away with his dirty hand.

Pain sliced through my skull like lightning as something hard hit the back of my head. Everything blurred into smears of colors. My legs gave way and I fell to the ground limp and defeated.

"Merick, take her to the prison wagon," a voice ordered as they dragged me outdoors.

My father's voice echoed somewhere in the distance begging for forgiveness. I saw the lightening sky through black bars and hard wood pressed into my back.

Everything spun, and darkness ate up my incoherent world.

❧

THE MERCY of the darkness didn't last long. The wagon rocked and shifted, each time sending a bolt of pain up my neck and into my head, rousing me and refusing to let me drift back into the refuge of unconsciousness.

I saw my village roll by. Men and women dressed in rags and mud pointed at me. Children catcalled. I wanted to hide my face, but what was the point? They all knew who I was. They all knew their worried-yet-salacious gossip of the miller's daughter's misfortunes had finally come true. My father had cost me my life.

A gauntlet rattled the bars, sounding out jarring, grating notes. I covered my ears, trying to lessen the pain throbbing at the base of my skull. Laughter quickly followed, and I saw it was the guard with dried blood crusted around his broken nose.

"Sleeping beauty finally wakes," he mocked. "Hope you're a lyin' one, 'cus I want to watch you burn for what you did to me."

"Shut up, Simon," the captain's stern voice ordered.

"Just havin' a bit of fun, that's all," Simon replied.

"Don't be such a little girl. It's just a broken nose. In fact, I think it improved your appearance," Merick added with a smirk.

Simon only scowled, throwing me one last murderous glare before walking farther up next to the mule.

Dirt roads turned into cobblestone streets. Hovels became houses with pretty thatched roofs that pointed towards the sky. The people were cleaner and more fashionable. But all of it—the grit and the gilt—fell under the shadow of the tall castle that greedily kept all the sun's rays to itself.

Terrifying towers surged into the heavens. A stagnant moat of black, oily water circled the thick stone and mortar walls. Soldiers looked down below from their posts, guard and menace all in one. Passing through the spiked castle gate was like being eaten by a monster, its yawning mouth growling open and its fangs clanging shut behind us.

People of all kinds scurried about the inner courtyard. Maids carried large wash baskets, while several men dressed in expensive doublets and colorful hose chatted as they strolled by, paying no attention to the new prisoner.

"Any educated man surely knows a war is about to be waged," a man opined, stroking his black mustache.

"If the educated man is a simpleton, then I would agree with your statement," his companion rebutted.

Their conversation melted into the background as we rolled past them.

I was jolted off balance at the wagon's abrupt stop. Through my prison bars I saw several ladies gliding before us, carefully lifting their skirts as they navigated through a maze of straw and dung. The guards were bewitched watching them float by. The women giggled, enjoying the admiration, the scent of citrus and flowers lingering behind them as they disappeared into the garden.

Looking down at my own dress of fraying homespun, I wondered how my life would have been different if I had been born a lady. I would have dresses of silk, pots of rouge, and exotic perfumes just like them. But what I envied most was their lack of hardship. They never had to work through the night to ensure their bellies would be full.

They never had to fear being turned out from their homes. They never had to worry at all.

"Get up!" Simon snarled, roughly pulling me from the cart.

I barely missed landing in a large pile of manure, the sour smell burning the insides of my nose.

"Afraid of a bit of muck, are we?" he laughed watching me clumsily tiptoe around the steaming pile. "Best get used to it, missy, 'cus you'll be shoveling the castle's supply if the king decides to deny you the mercy of death."

"Simon! Don't presume to know the king's judgments, or he'll have you scrubbing the cesspits with your wife's hair brush!" the captain snapped, coming up behind me and gripping my arm. "Return to the armory. I will bring the prisoner to his majesty."

I had to sprint to keep up with his long strides across the cobblestones. Grip still tight, he pushed me through a small door and up a narrow spiral staircase.

My lungs burned and sweat pooled between my breasts, my feet slipping several times on the worn steps. The coil of stairs seemed endless, but my tired heart leapt once we finally emerged, finding ourselves in one of the most beautiful rooms I had ever seen. Black and white tiles spread across the floor, while light streamed through stained glass windows. The ceiling dripped golds and reds, while colorful tapestries covered the walls. They bewitched me. Fabled princesses stood frozen in their floral realms, solemn expressions sewn eternally onto the faces. Brave knights offered salvation from beasts and monsters, rescuing their true loves from a dark fate.

I chuckled darkly to myself at such fairy tales. Bold knights didn't worry so much about the fate of women like me.

"One wrong word and it will be the last word you ever utter," the captain hissed, tightening his grasp on my arm. He straightened his posture, tugging at me to do likewise. A door opened, and a tall man strode into the room. The bejeweled crown sitting atop a mass of brown hair gave no doubt as to who he was.

King Edward was everything a king should be: a handsome face distinguished by piercing green eyes that showed a man with no use for patience. A few flecks of gray streaked his hair, but his neatly groomed beard remained a stark brown. He wore rich red robes, and his doublet was embroidered in gold thread nearly matching him to the ceiling.

"Rowan, why is she bound so tightly?" the king asked, his voice full of concern.

"Your majesty, she protested and struggled. It was the only way to ensure her obedience."

"Then you and your men are brutes," the king replied. "While I appreciate your fortitude, I do also appreciate that my goods not be damaged in transport. Especially ones so valuable. I've been waiting eagerly since I first got word last night about this exceptional discovery." He grimaced, inspecting the rope eating into my flesh. "Cut them off," he commanded.

I felt the quick kiss of cold metal between my wrists. Relief flooded my hands as the rope broke in two. The king gently took my hands in his and softly rubbed them to bring the blood back. I'd never been touched by anyone of higher birth, especially a king, and couldn't stop a wave of awkwardness from rushing over me.

"Be glad," he told Rowan as his thumb tenderly stroked the deep lines remaining on my wrists. "That this astonishing young woman has not been impaired by such force. Her hands must be venerated if they can truly do what I've been told. Otherwise I would ensure you met a similar fate, and I dare say no blood would ever find its way back into your fingers once I was satisfied you learned your lesson."

"Yes, your majesty," Rowan replied, coughing.

"Now, leave us," the king ordered.

The door creaked shut behind Rowan, and I was left alone with my monarch, further unease filling me as he continued to massage my wrists and hands.

"What is your name, dear child?" he asked, squeezing my palms gently.

"Laila, your majesty," I replied, trying to ignore his touch.

"Laila. Such a lovely name! When I heard about your exceptional skills, I never dreamt they would be contained within such beauty," he replied. "I suppose it is only correct for such a beautiful talent to mirror its owner."

His tender gaze turned stony and his grip suddenly tightened. My heartbeat pounded against his palms.

"It is treason not offering your gift to your king," he stated. "Did you honestly think you could remain hidden from me forever, your secret locked away? You think me an imbecile, don't you? A simpleton?"

His eyes dared me to refute him. Blood rushed through my ears, muffling his voice behind the pulsating sound of my own fear.

"Your majesty, I do not think any such thing," I answered slowly to keep my voice from shaking. "The story you have been told is only the fantasy of a drunk man trying to impress his friends. I have no hidden secret or special gift. I am only the daughter of a miller, a daughter betrayed by a father's lies. I am unable to spin straw into gold for your majesty, no matter how much I wish I could."

I prayed he would see reason, understand what everyone else until now had been unable to comprehend. Was the entire kingdom so easily fooled? He lowered his face to mine until his nose was not even an inch from my own, and said, "It sounds as though you are refusing. I am never refused."

"I am not refusing. It is simply impossible."

"Impossible?" he scoffed. "Yes, it may be impossible. In fact, it is most likely impossible. The problem is, I just don't believe you."

He was either mad or simply enjoyed the suffering of another. Either way, I wanted to get away from him. A sickly chill rolled through my stomach as he stroked my cheek, a smile imbued with something vile spreading over his face.

"I thought you might be unwilling to share your gift with me, not wanting to give your monarch the cut he deserves. But, there is always a way to discover genuineness. I can't abide lies of such stakes. A test is what you need, a simple one. Perhaps then you will succumb to my wishes and we will finally discover what is truth, and what is fable."

Pulling me across the tiled floor he flung back a velvet curtain hanging in the corner. There in the wall was a metal door, like one found in a prison. I shivered at the chill that went through my bones. The king removed a large brass key from his robes and fit it smoothly into the lock and opened the door.

He pushed me through and I found myself on yet another endless staircase, this one spiraling down. Torches lit the way until we reached the bottom. I looked around me and was filled with horror when I saw how exactly he intended to extract the truth he desired.

Straw.

Mountains of straw filled the room from floor to ceiling. Heavy stones crushed all hope. A rat scuttled along the wall's edge. Water dripped from small cracks. Darkness abounded except for the dim light from a small torch. In the center of the room, amid the golden slopes, stood a simple wooden spinning wheel. Baskets of empty bobbins were strewn all around, waiting to be filled by the girl who was supposedly able to spin straw into gold.

"I think it is very clear what I want you to do," the king hissed. "If by tomorrow morning you have not spun the straw into gold, well, I'm sure your head will fit quite nicely into one of these baskets instead."

My blood ran cold. It is one thing knowing you will die, but another completely to hear about the disposal of your remains.

"Spinning straw into gold is impossible! I could never do such a thing. No one can!" I pleaded.

"I suggest you figure it out. Spin for your freedom. That will be your prize. Otherwise, I will kill you and have your carcass nailed to a stake so the entire kingdom will see what I do to liars."

I grew dizzy and thought I might vomit. My limbs shook, and I couldn't stop thinking that death awaited me in the morning. I slumped against the spinning wheel, scrabbling to hold onto it and losing my footing as the wheel betrayed me and rolled, sending me stumbling into the straw. The king only laughed, and it made me hate him more than I knew possible.

"Don't look so glum! I know my methods may be harsh, but I do what's necessary to get the results I desire. You seem to need some motivation, and I have learned that death is the greatest motivation of all."

He gently ran a finger down my throat, "But I must admit, it would pain me greatly to sever such a beautiful neck."

My stomach twisted as a shiver ran through my body, blood

draining from my veins. I was forced to double over in agony, unable to breath. I wrapped my arms around my middle and dry heaved.

"Come, come, I'm sure it won't come to that," the king said, his lips cracked in a terrifying, gargoyle grin. "I suggest you focus your energy on the task at hand rather than self-pity if you want to be done by morning."

He departed, his shadow retreating behind him up the spiral staircase, leaving me alone to my kingdom of straw. A fresh wave of panic rippled through me as a thunderous bolt and lock echoed down from the iron door. I was sealed in. Entombed.

Frantically, I waded into the sea of straw to find a way out. One had to exist, it just had to be unearthed. A million sharp little ends pricked my skin, but the straw was too deeply packed against the walls for me to reach them. Refusing to surrender, I dove my hands within the thick jungle of twigs until I felt the cold stone beneath. I ran my hands quickly along the deep grooves of mortar, searching for some opening, some forgotten crevice that might lead to freedom. The needle-like straw bit my fingertips and scratched my hands until I stained the yellow twigs red with blood.

I would've kept searching until my hands were nothing but bone and sinew, the drive for survival hammering in my chest. However, as the hours passed, I finally began to accept the truth. There was no passage, no crevice, no way out except the heavy metal door atop the staircase.

I was completely trapped.

Resigned, I fell down into the straw. I put a hand to my neck, imagining the cold blade slicing my flesh, and then my head toppling down from the executioner's stand until it lay at the feet of the king. Lifting his trophy to a cheering crowd, he would remind them all of the penalty for boasting a lie.

The flicker of light danced across the treacherous landscape, my vision clouded by tears as the scenario played through my mind without end. Blade. Blood. Cheers.

If only my father had kept his mouth shut!

Wiping my eyes, I imagined the color of the straw growing more vibrant, the torchlight causing it to appear as burning flames.

My heart pounded. I saw a way to escape the fate chosen for me.

One spark from the torch would set the entire room ablaze, the inferno engulfing my body along with the mountains of straw, robbing the king the joy of his example.

I stared at the torch. The flames licked at the air, desiring to be fed. I could only imagine how quickly my skirts would ignite. Curious of the sensation of what burning to death would be like, I let my hand hover over the fire. Scorching pain flooded over my skin, causing me to gasp in surprise. It would be savage, but at least the results would be assured.

The king would return to nothing but ash.

It seemed such an easy thing to decide. Breathing slowly, I took the torch from the wall and marched towards the nearest hill of straw. The flames rejoiced at the feast waiting beneath them. Closing my eyes, I prepared to take destiny in my own hands. All I had to do was release my grip, and the nightmare would cease.

"Now why would you want to do a silly thing like that?" an amused voice asked behind me.

I spun around, shocked and confused as to who would be speaking to me in this locked cell. The torch slipped from my grasp and fell towards the straw, but a hand snatched it out of the air before it lit everything in flames.

"Determined to be stupid," the voice grumbled.

I expected to see one of the king's guards checking on my progress. Instead, I found a most peculiar man. He couldn't have been more than eight-and-twenty. Black hair framed a defined face with a pale complexion. He was tall but thin, wearing a tight fitting black doublet and pants. A white shirt peeked out of his collar and sleeves. Though his mouth smiled, his gray eyes held storms.

"Who...who are you?" I asked.

"Obviously someone who is keeping you from making a rather poor decision," he quipped, walking towards me with a firm step and placing the torch back where it belonged. "You must really hate it here to be so desperate to burn yourself up. You do know there are more pleasant ways to kill oneself?"

He stared at me, waiting for an answer. I was unable to reply, still trying to comprehend how this strange man was down here with me at all.

With a shrug, he moved past me over to the spinning wheel. He ran his long finger down the wheel, turning it and producing a happy purr from the machine.

"You see, I sensed you might be in need of some assistance. You must forgive the impertinence, but that's what I do, and by the looks of things, it appears my instincts were correct." His penetrating gaze chilled me.

"Are you here to rescue me?" I asked. It sounded stupid even as I said it, but I could see no other reasonable question to ask.

He laughed. "In a manner of speaking, though I think it might be in a different way than you are hoping."

In an instant, he was standing before me, my eyes hardly able to follow the speed with which he moved. My heart hammered in a new flush of panic. What sort of man was this?

Placing a hand over his own heart he gave a small bow, continuing, "I'm here to offer my services. I just happen to have quite the talent for spinning straw into gold."

For three seconds I felt I had been granted a miracle. But hard, cold reality stopped such foolishness, reminding me that this stranger's offer was not feasible.

"You mock me. How do you expect me to believe something so impossible?" I demanded. "No one can do that."

"You are the logical sort, aren't you? I like that," he said, nonchalantly plucking a twig from my hair, inspecting it under his slender nose. "If logic is what you desire, then you must realize it is already quite impossible that I am down here with you at all, and yet, here I am! I defy reason. Don't you think you at least owe me the courtesy to prove my skill?"

It aggravated me unreasonably that his point was valid. I hadn't heard one click of the lock or squeal of the hinges announcing his entrance. Somehow, he'd managed to appear out of thin air.

"All right," I agreed, still hesitant as to his means and motives, but viscerally curious to watch his reaction when he inevitably failed.

He was already positioned at the spinning wheel before the words left my mouth, stretching his fingers. There was not a single indication of doubt or trepidation in his manner. Poise emanated from him.

"Prepare to be dazzled," he smirked, removing a bobbin from one of the baskets and slipping it into place with an odd kind of delicacy. He sat down and began to pump his foot against the treadle, moving it slowly up and down. A smooth whirl hummed from the machine. The wheel spun faster and faster until the wooden spokes disappeared completely. Keeping a steady rhythm, he grabbed a handful of straw and fed it into the rotating mouth, the twigs twisting together and threatening to break. Unconcerned he grabbed more straw, nourishing the small rope of twigs forming in his hands until the rope became taut, gold glinting between his white fingers.

He stopped the wheel and spun around in his chair, triumph on his face as he pulled off the bobbin and dangled a twinkling golden thread in front of my nose.

"Maybe this will teach that logical brain of yours to believe the impossible," he said, watching as I touched the string in amazement.

"It's gold! It's real gold," I said in wonder, seeing my salvation in every inch. "Thank you. You've saved my neck and my life."

The golden thread in the palm of his hand vanished, and the storms in his eyes grew darker. He took a small step back, his black boots crunching the straw beneath them.

"It's true I don't want to let a poor, innocent girl fall prey to the king's greed," he frowned. "But be warned, my help comes with a price."

Unease wrinkled its way back into my joy. I couldn't help but cling to this wild new hope, but I also knew–all too well–that no one did anyone a kindness simply out of goodness.

"I don't know what I can give to repay for such a service," I replied feeling down my tattered skirts, praying I might find a rogue coin or two even though I knew I had none. "I have no money."

He smiled reassuringly.

"Lucky for you, money does not interest me," he said as he circled me, his gaze traveling up and down my body until it rested on my neck. My cheeks grew hot at being observed with such intensity, wondering which of several unsavory options he could be considering.

"That necklace is quite stunning," he complimented, his fingers grazing my skin as he lifted the pendent to examine it. "Yes, this is quite nice." He let it drop. "How about you give me your trinket, and in return I'll fix this little problem of yours?"

I clutched the pendant. It was a family relic. I'd worn it every moment since my mother died. She had given it to me, just as her mother had given it to her.

"This was my mother's," I replied, looking down at the golden orb, a constellation of rubies speckled around its circumference. "I don't know if I could ever part with it. Surely you can accept something else?"

"I'm afraid you've overestimated my generosity," he replied icily. "The choice is yours to make. You can either keep the little sentimental piece of metal and wear it proudly to the gallows, or you can trade it for something far more valuable. Your life."

He held out his open palm, a sly smile crossing his lips.

The pendant in my hand weighed as heavy as my soul. I fumbled with it between my fingers, stupidly hoping he would reconsider.

"I'm afraid my patience is wavering. I don't enjoy wasting my time with the indecisive," he said with a sigh. "Do you choose life or death? Honestly, a simpler choice has never been made."

I had to make my decision and I would do whatever it took to survive the king's greed.

His anticipation was electric as I touched the pendant one final time, unclasping the hook and letting it drop into his exposed palm. The chain coiled like a snake before he closed his fingers over it, the necklace vanishing instantly. He regarded my surprise with a satisfied smirk.

"Excellent," he said, walking back to the spinning wheel. "Now that boring business is out of the way, we can really have some fun! Besides, precious minutes are just flying by, and we don't want to risk angering the king, do we?"

I shook my head, watching as he turned his full attention to the machine before him, grinning. Just as before his foot pumped the treadle up and down, forcing the wheel to spin as he fed handfuls of straw into the rotating mouth. A thin gold thread wound itself rapidly around the bobbin, running from side to side until the entire spool was full faster than I had known possible. Then he threw the filled bobbin into the basket and grabbed another, repeating the process again.

Grab, spin, throw.

He paid no attention to the strands of black hair falling in front of his eyes, or his breaths, which grew labored. Rhythm consumed him.

Grab, spin, throw.

I stood mesmerized, watching him work. The rotation never ceased, the straw turning to gold between his fingers, agile hands releasing and repositioning a fresh spool quicker than I could catch. It was violent, and yet beautiful at the same time.

"Why don't you make yourself useful and fetch me some straw instead of gawking at me." His voice broke through my reverie. "I should be very grateful if I can have this finished before winter."

"Yes, of course—right away."

I grabbed one of the empty baskets and started filling it with several armfuls of straw.

I don't know how many I placed by his side, but it seemed an endless amount. Every time I would leave him the pile would be high, and when I returned not moments later, it was already gone. Sweat broke across my forehead, but I forced myself to keep up with him. He worked more diligently than anyone I'd ever witnessed, yet he showed no signs of fatigue. In fact, quite the opposite. It was as if the spinning empowered him. Made him glow more brightly. He made me feel lazy by comparison, and I never shirked from intense labor.

Slowly, the mountains of straw shrunk into hills, and then into mounds as I watched spool upon spool fill with gold. The baskets began overflowing, causing him to resort to simply tossing the filled bobbins any which way.

"I wonder what the king has planned with so much gold?" he asked, flinging the final spool against the wall beside him, a loud crack reverberating across the floor. "Hopefully he will use it towards something remotely useful, like remodeling this castle. Do you realize how old fashioned a dungeon is these days?"

I couldn't help but smile, imagining the king spending his wealth on such a project, let alone choosing fabric and debating where the furniture should be placed.

"Yes, but I dare say anyone he hires for such a thing will have a better chance of becoming a part of the foundation than receiving payment," I joked, feeling as if I was finally catching my breath from all the miserable and miraculous surprises of the past day.

For a moment, he shared in my amusement, a flicker of delight dancing across his gaze. It was short-lived. The cool exterior he wore so elegantly returned and only grew colder. He stood from the wheel and brushed a few specks of straw debris off his shirt.

"Now that your head is safe, I fear I must I be off," he said.

"Wait!" I cried, "What is your name? I must know. You've saved me this night, and I will be forever grateful."

He stopped, his shoulders rolling back and remaining stiff. He turned his head and said, "I am nothing but a good-hearted stranger."

With that, he vanished, leaving behind no trace he had ever been there except for the gold surrounding me. Had I blinked? He was there, and then simply...not.

What sort of being was I dealing with?

CHAPTER TWO

THE SECOND DAY: LAILA

The **king stood** in absolute silence, his eyes caressing the sight of the towers of gold encircling us. Each spool was more radiant than the next. Dumbfounded, he picked a heavy spool from the nearest stack and slowly unwound the golden thread around his finger to inspect the miracle before him.

"It's genuine. All of it. Your father wasn't a liar after all," he said before he bit the thread between his teeth. "I told you my methods produce results. I am happy you saw reason and succumbed to my wishes rather than remain defiant. Isn't it much simpler this way?"

He caressed the spool lovingly. Watching him made me feel ill, even though my stomach protested its lack of food in the past day. Taking great care, he placed it back among his new collection, his gaze moving away from the glitter to meet my own.

"You are truly a marvel, a bright star that is beautiful to behold, dear Laila. Such a pure and brilliant talent flows through you," he said, taking my hands within his and bestowing a kiss. I could feel the prickle of his beard, the sensation rough and foreign. I wanted to rip away from him, but I thought it wise not to attempt such a bold move. He wavered between insane and benign too closely and too quickly.

"As I have pleased your majesty and done what you asked, may I now return to my mill?" I spoke instead, disgusted by the wet patches he left after each kiss.

His grip tightened at my words. Damn.

"Return? But my dear, you've spun so little gold this night. You can't expect me to allow someone of such miraculous skill to leave? No, that wouldn't do. Not yet anyway," he stated bluntly.

My breathing hitched. Should I really have expected anything else from such a lunatic? My towers of hope came crashing down around me even as he gazed at his towers of gold yet again.

"But I spun your gold, I should be freed. That was what you told—"

"You will spin as much as I desire," he snapped back. "If you refuse, I will make sure the executioner's blade is exceptionally dull, so every strike he must take to hack through that pretty neck of yours will be agony."

He grazed my collarbone with hot fingertips.

"This gold you've spun is quite impressive to be sure, but I fear it is just a taste of the true bounty you will afford my kingdom. Tonight your delicate fingers will work their magic once more, and they will continue to do so until I am satisfied."

I wanted to scream, to fight, to bash one of those heavy spools into his greasy temple until his skull cracked like an egg, its sick yolk spilling out onto the stones. But all I could do was nod in obedience. I didn't want to antagonize his madness further.

"Excellent," he said. "Now the only question is what to do with you until everything is prepared."

He grabbed my chin, turning my head to the right, then left. I wanted to ask him if he wished to count my teeth like a proper buyer of a horse.

"It is a shame such beauty is hidden by a layer of grime and muck," he said, his tone thick with lust.

He released my jaw.

"Don't worry, my dear, there is no need for alarm. I am not a complete monster," he chuckled, wiping a smear of dirt from my cheek. "In fact, I believe you deserve a bit of pampering for your labor. Perhaps a bath? And a new dress. Yes. A girl always loves a new dress."

He wrapped his fingers around my wrist and pulled me along back towards the stairs. As we ascended I couldn't help but look back at the empty spinning wheel, knowing it would not be long until the room was replenished with straw, needing to be spun into gold.

My thoughts fell immediately to the stranger who had saved my life. But would he come again? I hardly knew how he had "sensed it" as he said the first time. My mind started reeling with each step trying to figure it out. There had to be some way to contact him, but how?

LIGHT STREAMED through stained glass windows as we emerged from the dungeon. I couldn't help but notice the exquisite tapestries again as we passed through the maze of hallways. The princesses were still frozen, and the knights continued to rescue them from fabled threats. They were the same, and in a way, I felt a measure of their glamor. For had I not faced death and been rescued at the last minute by a powerful stranger?

I felt for my necklace as I always did in times I needed strength, but as I rubbed naked skin I remembered it was gone. The princesses' hollow eyes knew what I was just beginning to understand. Salvation came at a price.

The king stopped at the end of the hall and opened a door. I was determined to despise whatever it would be. I wanted nothing from him but the freedom he promised. But when my eyes fell on the room, I forgot my angry words and frantic fight.

It was the most beautiful, luxurious room I had ever seen. Persian rugs, gilt furniture, and a proper bed filled a space larger than the entire hovel I had called home. Stunned, I stared at the fine fabrics and filigreed fripperies surrounding me.

"Beautiful, isn't it? I thought it might please you," the king said with shining eyes. "I told you I wasn't such a dragon as all that."

Unable to stop myself, I ran my hand down one of the wooden posts of the bed. The mattress was not a mat of molding straw and rough linen, but filled to bursting with actual feathers. Pillows covered in silk waited enticingly. My body ached to know the sensation of such comfort.

"Your majesty," a small voice piped behind us.

A plump older woman stood in the doorway, waiting for orders. Her face flushed red as the king motioned her to enter.

"I want you to make sure she is well rested and refreshed for tonight," he told the woman. "And, good God, give her a decent gown to wear. I can't stand to look at something so poor any longer. It makes me ill."

She bowed. I knew my appearance was far from refined, but I doubted that mind of his could be any more ill than it already was. Taking my hand, he placed one last kiss upon it, sending a shiver of hatred down to my toes. Then he left, and I was alone with the woman, who was clucking at me in disapproval.

"My what a vision, or perhaps nightmare is more like it!" she exclaimed grabbing me and forcefully turning me around. "Will take quite a bit of work, this will. Such awful tangles! But, I think you'll clean up quite nicely once I'm through with you."

Immediately, thick fingers pulled out pieces of straw from my hair. She squinted as she roved over every lock on my head, making sure she extracted every last fragment with a surgeon's skill. Once satisfied, she pulled me into an adjoining room, where a large copper bath filled with steaming water stood in the middle. I watched in awe as she poured a pitcher of milk, flower petals and several drops of fragrant oil in the water.

The fragrance was tempting, and it made my determination to hate the king's sick generosity all the more difficult.

"Come now, don't be shy," she said kindly.

The water lapped enticingly against the metal tub. She removed my clothes, nasty remarks about the state of each garment whispered under her breath.

Looking again at the milky water with a frown, I slowly dipped my foot in. Immediately the sensation of warmth flowed over my body. It was everything I feared it would be...glorious.

Sinking further into the soft scents of lavender and rose, I momentarily forgot that death eagerly awaited me. I forgot that I was only a peasant, the daughter of a drunk. For that brief moment, I was one of those ladies floating through the courtyard, men bowing reverently as I gracefully passed by.

I was a princess.

I was a queen.

THE SECOND DAY: RUMPELSTILTSKIN

"N**othing but a** good hearted stranger."

That is what I had told her. If she knew the truth about my heart, I doubt she would find my company so agreeable.

I held her necklace between my fingers, tiny rubies twinkling like stars in a miniature night sky. Though a tad sentimental, she was quite a curious creature.

When I first appeared before her, I expected to find her strewn across a bed of straw, arms flailed behind her head, a river of tears flowing into a pool by her side. Instead, she stood over those dried twigs, a torch gripped in hand hovering menacingly above its feast. I couldn't help but find this reaction beguiling. Not every girl is willing to burn herself to death simply to spite a king. That's a spirit and sentiment I could heartily approve.

I coiled the necklace into a box and stored it away. There were more important things I needed to attend to besides pondering suicidal women, such as the king's predictable demand for more gold.

His greed would ultimately be his ruin. I had provided the first maddening taste. Now all I had to do was allow nature to take its inevitable course. It was beautiful to witness. He would pay a thousand times over with everything he held dear for what he had done to me.

I walked towards the window. Moonlight streamed in through the rippled pane of crown glass, illuminating the room with its cool glow. I opened the window to the night, breathing the chilled air with a deep hunger for despair.

My predatory heart pounded, feeding on the insatiable hunger that was driving me to the inevitable moment when Laila's name would belong to me. She had to sign it away, of course, but, I had no doubt she would happily bind herself to my pretty lies.

Closing my eyes and allowing my hunger to sharpen and stretch out, I searched for her. Though the sky was black I could easily see the entire landscape of the kingdom reveal itself to me. Rolling hills divided into a patchwork of fields before they bled into the stark buildings of the town. None of that interested me except for the little pinpoints of light floating like fireflies below. They glowed brightly, some moving like blood through the veins of the streets, while others congealed in the homes. Each was a tragic soul, their desperate flames tempting me to offer them something better. Going higher, I rose above them. Tonight, there was only one flame I cared about.

Great turrets surged upwards, breaking the monotonous night sky as the castle came into view, the little flames walking hurriedly within its walls. They didn't notice the thing watching them, seeping into every crack and crevice, searching for the girl who wished it could all be but a bad dream. My heart quickening as I heard a low tone rise from the depths of the castle. A sad refrain vibrated between angry and terrified, but the bass note was pure desperation.

Dear little Laila was calling to me.

Once again, it was time for me to save the day.

A VISION of terrifying beauty stood before me.

An ocean of flaxen twigs engulfed the floor. Golden waves crashed against pillars and walls. Every surface was washed by the roiling surf except for the small island where Laila stood like Andromeda chained to her rock, waiting for the monster...or me, as was the case.

What truly caught my attention was her transformation. She no longer resembled the ragged little thing I first encountered, but was now some great beauty that held herself in a way that was nearly regal. The wild strands had been tamed into a cascading braid of chestnut, and a gown of blue velvet swathed her in twilight hues. She flushed becomingly as her well-supported bosom rose and fell with each breath.

Those bloody boring baser instincts of my body stirred at the sight of her delectable décolletage, but I shook it off. I had work to do. Besides, I was a gentleman, at least when I was given the chance to be.

"It looks like our dear monarch has become quite the patron of your craft," I snickered. "He's even gone to the trouble of giving you a room double the size of last night. How very considerate of him!"

"You've returned!" she exclaimed, whirling around to face me.

"Of course I've returned. You can't think me so rude as to abandon you when your lovely head is still on the line?" I asked, placing a hand over my heart feigning insult. "That just wouldn't be right."

Her dress was cut low, leaving little to the imagination, and I could plainly see her breasts rising with another deep breath as she studied me. I wished she would put them away. Their distraction was a damned nuisance.

I looked around the room, trying to calculate how much gold all the straw would become. The sum I came up with was enormous. I was impressed by just how much the king's greed had blossomed since the night before.

"Whatever has he required of you this time? Wait. Let me guess. More gold, perhaps?"

She twisted her gown in her hands, and something like resentment stiffened her features.

"The king demands this entire room be spun into gold before dawn. If not, well, you already know." Her voice was hollow.

"I wish the king would be more imaginative with his punishments. It's always death for this and death for that. Death is so boring!" I groaned, rolling my eyes and shaking my head.

"Death is not boring when your life is the one being threatened," she snapped. "You are a callous man, or whatever you *are*, to be so droll at a time like this."

"My, my. You have a nice set of claws you keep hidden with that pretty new manicure," I replied, circling her slowly. "But, I would recommend you not antagonize the only one willing and able to help you. It looks like there is quite a lot more work to be done tonight, and I'm beginning to wonder if I even feel up to it. And for your information, I am...very much a man, I just happen to have a few improvements over my peers."

Her lips tightened, as if to keep hasty words from coming out, words that might lead me to disappear along with all her hope of survival.

"I'm sorry for my outburst," she said finally. "I'm so rattled between fear and anger that I don't know what's up or down."

"Don't apologize." I stopped in front of her. "In fact, you had better harness some of that anger if you wish to survive this adventure. That brings to mind...however did you achieve getting yourself in this odd predicament?"

"My father. He boasts and brags, telling lies that have imperiled us more than once. He is the reason I have to spin straw into gold. The bastard betrayed me, all to impress a few drunks and save his own neck."

I was no stranger to the pain in her tone. It poisoned me, its bitter taste lingering behind every word. I almost felt sorry for her.

Almost.

"You are in luck, as I'm feeling quite generous today. I suppose I can spare the time to help you again," I said.

She opened her arms, as if hoping to launch herself into my embrace. Not wanting to engage in anything so frivolous, I put out a cautioning hand, stopping her dead in her tracks.

"Not so fast," I stated. "You might want to hear my conditions before you decide to garland me with such affection. Tempting as it might be, I cannot simply spin this all for free. What will you give me for my efforts?"

She looked bewildered, her hand instinctively touching her now naked neck.

"I gave you my necklace. I don't have anything of value left to give you," she said, trembling.

I chuckled at her.

"Now if that were true, I can say for certain I would not be here. You still have something I would consider quite valuable," I whispered, nearing her, seeing the glint of silver on her finger. "How about that lovely ring?"

I could sense the bite of my words as her expression turned from worried to sorrowful. I knew it was all she had left of her dear, dead Mummy, but it had to be done.

"This is all I have left of my mother," she whimpered, a sob threatening at any moment. "It's of no value to you."

"You're honestly going to let a scrap of silver stand in the way of saving your life? Come, I know you are smarter than that."

I held out my hand just as I had done the previous night and waited.

I didn't have to wait long until cool resignation washed over her. She twisted the band from her finger and held it out to me, looking away.

I gleefully took it, plucking it from her fingers and rolling the ring around in my palm.

"I can assure you mothers prefer their children live rather than cling to a memento in a gruesome death on the scaffold."

She refused to meet my gaze.

"Now that's settled," I announced, stretching my hands, "I suppose it best we begin."

I sat down at the spinning wheel, my fingertips enjoying the wood's familiar smooth grain. I pumped my foot up and down, the treadle easily giving way to my direction until I reached the correct speed.

I grabbed a handful of straw from the nearest pile and fed the long strands into the bobbin, the wheel whirring happily with each mouthful it consumed. However, I quickly noticed the pile was getting lower and was not replenished as it should have. That's when I heard a mournful sniffle coming from behind me.

I smiled to myself.

I turned around, seeing Laila with red, watery eyes. I usually didn't acknowledge such displays of tawdry emotion. Tears had little effect on me. But right now, they were the prospect I most desired. I shuffled the cards and played my hand, keeping my ace well hidden.

"For a grown woman you certainly behave as a child," I scoffed. "Crying is a waste. You'll never solve your problems if this is the best you can do."

Redness rushed across her chest and cheeks.

"Being nasty won't do anything for that hole in your chest, either," she spat back.

"Now that's more like it," I beamed.

She crossed her arms, spite wrinkling her pert little nose.

"What am I supposed to do now?" she asked hotly. "The king is a madman and you only take odd heirlooms of which I have no more. I am dead. I see that now. He is only going to want more and more and I can give no more."

"May I offer you some advice that might quell these waterworks of yours?" I asked. "You are allowing your frantic sorrow to blind you. There is an opportunity presenting itself before you, but you refuse to quit your moaning and grasp it by the throat. You may think you are as tough as leather, but you are really just as weak as wool."

She laughed like I was cracked, her throat still rough with tears.

"What could possibly be an opportunity? Prison? Torture? Yes, those are all great opportunities that I should joyfully embrace."

I let out a dramatic sigh. She had a lot to learn about the art of influence.

"Only if you play your cards wrong," I replied. "First, you are right...the king will never release you. That hope died the moment he saw the first thread of gold. But that doesn't mean you can't create for yourself a better situation than life in a cell or without a head. You need to realize you are the one offering what he wants most. That means it's you that has the power, not him."

"What do you mean?" she asked. Despite her pique, I could see her eyes widening with cautious interest.

"*I mean*, you should try to gain something more than your measly little life. Make him offer you something for his reward. Make him see you will be much more valuable if he shows a bit more kindness to you. I never work for free, and neither should you. It's the most fundamental principle of commerce!"

"It is a principle dependent on a wild card. You," she said, pointing her pretty finger at me.

"Have I let you down so far?" I asked with a shrug.

"No, but didn't you hear? I have nothing left to give you. It is over."

"Don't be so quick to damn yourself. Let me be the judge of when that will be. For right now, I think it best not to worry about all that. I have found there is always a price one is willing to pay."

I could see her thinking, trying to figure it out, still not completely convinced.

"It will never work. He would kill me for treason if I refused to spin," she said.

I shook my head in disappointment at her shortsightedness.

"Stop being such a dolt! Don't you understand? You are too valuable to kill. He won't do it. He might huff and puff, but he knows a good thing when it passes him by."

She twisted her gown in her hands once again. Standing up, I walked towards her, our bodies merely a breath from one another. I pulled the soft fabric away from her cold fingers and placed her hands at her sides.

"You have more power than you give yourself credit for," I said, gazing down at her.

She laughed that throaty laugh again.

"What I have is pain."

I stifled the grin threatening to spread across my lips.

"Ahhh, then you have the most valuable commodity there is. Pain is power, my dear. Don't you know?"

"How is that power? How can such festering do anything but cause me suffering?"

"That's a simpleton's question. You have a lot to learn if that's how you see it."

I leaned in, expecting her to turn her head away from my gaze, but she remained frustratingly firm. I turned my head instead. I was far too close to plump lips and fragrant skin, and I could not afford to lose myself even for a moment in arousal's sweet trap.

"Close your eyes," I commanded in her ear.

Her lids snapped shut, but she crossed her arms defiantly.

"Now, since you can't see it for yourself, let me help you. I want you to summon up a moment, one where your pain was greatest."

"My mother's death, I suppose," she breathed.

"*I suppose* isn't good enough. It either is, or it isn't."

She sighed and twisted her face.

"Think! You mentioned your father, how he deceived you. Tell me, what happened?"

My fingers grazed her skirts, rubbing the nap of the velvet the wrong way simply to feel it and to ground myself. I waited, but again I was met with nothing but insufferable silence. Then she spoke with a clarity and strength in her voice I hadn't heard before.

"He couldn't put me first," she stated. "He'd rather impress those drunken prunes at the tavern then sustain our livelihood."

"Good. Go on," I pushed, my heart pumping excitedly for what I yearned to fall from her lips. My hands brushed against her waist, the hard ribs of the corset under the bodice exciting me with the thought of how they contained and constrained her.

"I told him not to boast. I told him one day it would destroy us. But he didn't listen. He didn't care. He had to uphold his honor at the cost of mine." Every word of hers was now exact and resonant. "He told them I could spin straw into gold. And the king believed him, believed a drunk! What kind of idiot believes a drunk? What kind of father waves his daughter like a red cloth before a bull?"

Her tears were gone.

"How did it make you feel?" I asked, savoring the power radiating from her, inhaling her energy even as my own breath vanished when I touched the edge of her bodice where velvet met skin.

"Betrayed." There was no hesitation in this word. "He might as well have put his hand inside my chest and crushed my heart. That moment refuses to die. It repeats endlessly in my brain, forcing me to remember every cruel detail. Reminding me what I wish not to admit."

"And what is that?"

Her hands clenched into fists as her heart continued to bleed. I struggled against the slight trembling in my own hands as I traced the tops of her breasts and the column of her throat.

"Everything was taken from me. My last hopes, my dreams. I was destined to live in poverty and fear. I hate him! I hate my father! I hate the king and his madness!"

"Excellent! Don't stop. What is it you want?" The line of her jaw was iron encased in ivory silk, and I had the most unaccountable urge to lick it from chin to ear.

"I want to choose my own fate, and not let it be determined by such a waste of men. I want to be fearless like those women I saw in the courtyard when they brought me here in bonds. If I can't have my freedom, then I want to be queen."

"Then that is exactly what you demand," I whispered, stroking her bottom lip with a feather-light caress of my thumb. "Harness that pain, take hold of the power you now feel flowing through your veins. Make your fate your own."

Her eyes flashed open and she looked at me as if for the first time. I was witnessing a rebirth, and it was more beautiful than I ever hoped.

"When have tears ever given you such a sensation?" I asked, keeping my voice low and persuasive.

"Never," she stated, the word filled with strength.

"Then I won't be bothered by them anymore?"

She smiled, and the darkness that now shadowed her eyes made me absolutely giddy. I wanted to bite those plump lips that were curved into such a wicked, wanton grin.

"No," Laila said with supreme serenity only hatred and power can grant. "I don't want them clouding my vision. I want to see the king's face as I take his power from him."

"Beautifully said," I complimented. "Nothing would give me greater joy than to have you receive this gift."

Her expression stiffened, and her body lengthened as if already trying her new regal air. I lengthened in response, though I fiercely swore this was only because her newfound power was as intoxicating as any aphrodisiac.

"You swear if I make this demand of the king, you will spin for me one last time?"

My heart leapt.

"You have my word," I said.

I put out my hand and she immediately gripped it firmly. The sensation burned as hotly as if I had thrown her down in the straw and made it catch fire with my power and her passion. But, I knew better than to fall prey to lust, and most of all I knew that it was hatred that bound us, not love. It was hatred that would ensure that together, we would bring about the king's ruin.

And my revenge would be sweeter than any lady's charms could ever be.

CHAPTER THREE

Distaff:

noun: A cleft stick attached to a spinning wheel, used for holding the wool or flax the spinner will need.

adjective: Of or concerning women.

THE LONG-DEAD PAST: CHILD OF PAIN

Pain found me easily.

It festered in my heart. Bubbled every time a door slammed in my face, or each time my stomach growled with hunger. Cold stares, pointing fingers and a chorus of whispers never let me forget what I had become.

"That's the boy," they would say. "Don't want the likes of him around. Bad family. Nothing but trouble."

A kick or jeer would often follow, furthering my growing distrust of people even though I couldn't blame them. Not when I brought danger to their door. No one wanted to incur the king's wrath, which is what would happen if it was ever discovered they took in the boy he had ordained to be an eternal outcast.

I hated the king. Hated him with every fiber of my being for what he made me become, what he did to my family. He took everything, leaving me only my name, tainted by treachery.

But, I endured, though I sometimes wondered why I bothered. Eventually, I found hope in the form of three spinsters. The Pythin Sisters made a livelihood of spinning the wool from their small herd of sheep. As luck would have it, I discovered they were in need of an extra set of hands about their small farm.

No one wanted to associate with them. Stories of hidden gold, an unhealthy taste for whiskey and even witchcraft lingered in their wake. While these tales put most people off, to me, it offered a direction to follow. I needed desperate people, and who better than three sisters embroiled in simmering scandal?

On a blustery day, I set off from the poor shelter of the dead elm tree trunk I had been sleeping in. The path was rocky and uneven, making it difficult to keep my balance as the wind blew against me. Winter was trying to proclaim dominance over the kingdom, its icy breath sealing the earth with a fine frost.

I never saw anything so whimsical as the Pythin Sisters' house. It was like a clockmaker and an artist had an argument after a long night of drinking. Gray stones were puzzle-pieced together, and the thatched roof looked on the verge of collapse at any moment.

The place felt eerie and abandoned. The bleating of the sheep carried on the wind as they peacefully grazed on the rolling hills. My fingers were nearly frozen through as I banged loudly on the battered door, the old boards groaning from my assault.

No answer. I tried again.

I stepped back to turn around when the door flung open. Three pairs of green eyes in three faces framed by a rainbow of frizzy hair looked straight at me.

Clownishly red, white blonde, and black curls bounced every which way. The women were neither young nor old, wearing loose dresses fastened tightly around the middle with multi-colored stays.

"What do you want?" the brunette sister asked, eyeing me narrowly.

"I heard you are in need of help and I wanted to offer my services," I answered.

"A bit scrawny, if you ask me, Mina. And so pale!" the redhead chimed in, her nose wrinkling in disapproval. "Couldn'a be more than eight or ten years old."

"Nothin' that can't be undone with a little care, Edna," the blonde responded, a reassuring smile appearing on her pink lips. "Besides, no one else has come around. Beggars can't be choosers."

Mina waved at them to be quiet. "What's your name, boy?"

I closed my eyes, bracing myself for a kick or a lash for having dared darkened their doorway.

"Rumpelstiltskin, ma'am," I said, resisting the urge to preemptively shield myself from the coming blows.

None came.

"He's the traitor's boy," the blonde whispered. "It might be dangerous to take him."

"True, Alma," Mina said. "But we are too old to do the work ourselves, and there is little chance of anyone else wanting to risk their reputation associating with us. At least this boy has no reputation to lose."

I prayed as she considered me closely, her sisters murmuring in both her ears. I prepared myself for the inevitable, looking out at a land that was as barren as my future.

After a few more moments of deliberation, Mina gestured for them to quiet, her face filled with a compassion I had not seen since my mother.

"A name doesn't determine who you are," she said, smiling. "We will allow you to stay."

My heart leapt with gratitude.

"You'll really take me? Even knowing my name?" I asked, breathless.

"We believe in fate, my young child," she said. "There is a reason you have come here. It would be wrong to turn you away. Besides, we really do need the help."

Six hands reached out and pulled me through the door. Inside, a crackling fire greeted me with its warmth. Blood rushed to my fingers and cheeks, reviving my nearly frozen flesh. I was drawn to the cozy chairs by the fireplace, though my eyes catalogued the odd trinkets tucked into even odder corners.

Of the hundreds of curious objects sticking out of crevices, smashed between books, and even poking out of flowerpots, my attention settled on a large ball of glass sitting motionless upon black velvet.

"What's that?" I asked, walking to the crystal and eyeing its smooth surface.

"Edna! You forgot to cover the crystal again!" Mina scolded. "Brainless girl! You know you can't leave it out in the elements."

"It allows one to see into another's future, allowing us brief moments we can interpret in order to guide them through the murkiness that lies in their paths," Alma interjected.

"How does it work?" I asked. The clarity of the glass mesmerized me.

"I'm afraid you are much too young to know its secrets," Alma said, covering the ball. "Besides, it is more important you focus on your work. There is much to be done."

Taking me by the shoulder, they guided me through the house. The wooden floor creaked and buckled with each step, as if it were a living thing. The tour was punctuated by information and warnings.

"This is the kitchen," Edna said, motioning to a large oven that looked like it needed a good cleaning.

"Here are our rooms, not to be entered, mind you," Mina said. The other two made a grimace only the bravest of men would challenge.

"There is a room with a wash basin and tub down that hall," Edna said quickly as I was shuffled along.

"And here is where you will sleep," Mina said smiling, pointing up a ladder to a high loft.

I looked at the rickety ladder, unsure if it would hold my weight. Closing my eyes, I took my first step, the wood giving off a menacing creak.

"Give me a hand, would you dear?" Edna asked from below once I was up a few rungs. "I'm not as spry as I once used to be."

Her fingerless glove was scratchy against my palm as I pulled her up. Then, to my horror, the other two started up behind her as well, completely unfazed by the possibility of us all plummeting to our deaths, or at the very least, some broken bones.

"Don't let it bother you, my dear," Mina said. "The ladder might be a tad temperamental, but it is still quite sturdy. Once it gets to know you, you won't have to worry about a thing."

I breathed a sigh of relief once we reached the top. The loft was distinctive from the whimsy below. Plain walls enclosed a large, mostly bare space.

Alma struck a match and started lighting several small lanterns. They twinkled like stars in the darkness.

"I know it isn't the fanciest of situations, but at least it will be warm. The heat from the fire loves to rise up here. I almost feel dreamy just thinking about it!" Mina reassured. "There is a straw mattress over there and an old quilt folded over in that wardrobe. Mind you, it might be a bit dusty and need an airing out on the morrow."

There could have been icicles hanging from the ceiling, and I still wouldn't have minded. I was simply happy to have a place to sleep other than the outdoors.

In the far corner, I saw the most peculiar object yet. A large wooden wheel sat propped up on a sort of stand, a cloud of wool stuck on a spike at the front.

"This is where we spin," Alma announced, noticing my interest. "On the spinning wheel," she added.

"A wheel that spins?" I said dumbly. "But, don't all wheels go round?"

Laughing at my naiveté, Alma took a seat behind the wooden wheel. She picked up the wool and began to methodically work the pedal with her foot. Spinning madly round and round, the large spokes blurred together until they nearly looked invisible. The wool ran through her fingers effortlessly as the spool gobbled the white fluff.

"See, it's quite easy!" she exclaimed, grabbing another ball of wool and feeding it to the insatiable beast. "It's all in the tension."

"Oh dear, he still looks a bit befuddled!"

"Maybe we went too fast?"

"Sit here, dear," Edna ordered, nudging Alma out of the way. She gave me a gentle push and plopped me down into the empty seat.

"Now, you take this wool here," she said, putting a wad of it in my hand. "And place your right foot on the treadle below. Now push it up and down, up and down, until you feel the rhythm in your bones. That's it. Grip the wool firmly and stretch it into the bobbin. Not so much, now! Yes, much better."

"He learns quickly, this one!"

"What talent!"

Whirr! Whirr! Whirr!

The rhythm of the wheel merged with my body, and for a moment my mind was cleansed. There was only repetition. Continuous motion. My pulse beat along with the treadle. The fibers ran through my fingers in a constant stream. I liked it.

"That's enough for today," Edna finally said, placing her hand on the wheel and breaking my concentration. "I dare say he would go on all night if we let him!"

"Should make life much easier for us," Mina replied.

The other two agreed happily with her.

"But, there is more to this job than just spinning, I'm afraid," Edna continued. "As with all pleasures in life, there is decidedly less pleasant work to be done first."

TRUE TO HER WORD, the less pleasant work started early the next morning, but unlike every other morning of my life, I was able to go at it warmly clad, with a full belly, and rested from a good night of sleep. The sun was barely peeking over the horizon when I went out into the cool morning air, carrying two armfuls of alfalfa.

"The sheep are your first priority. The number one thing you must do is give them nourishment," Alma said. "The pasture here is not quite up to snuff in these cold months."

As I opened the gate, hungry bleats scolded me for making them wait. Between the slick muck beneath my feet and the army of warm noses prodding my back and legs, it was a miracle I didn't fall. But I completed the chore without complaint. I was handed a shovel.

"After they are fed their stall must be cleaned. Make sure you put down a nice layer of thick straw after. They get frightfully grumpy if you skimp on their straw."

Two empty buckets.

"Make sure the troughs are filled. You need to check on their water several times a day. If the ice freezes the surface, take a pickaxe to it and give it hell," Edna instructed.

Another hundred little tasks soon followed, each one preventing me from doing the one thing I wanted to do. Spin.

After dodging a head-butt from a particularly irritable sheep as I trimmed her hoof, I finally saw Mina come out to let me know I had earned my lunch.

Sitting in the kitchen, I noticed I was alone. Stuffing the bread and cheese in my mouth, I took my chance. I went back up the loft, where the wheel stood all alone. Everything was just as it was left the day before. It was beautiful.

Just as I put out an eager hand to touch the smooth grain, a disapproving cluck echoed behind me.

"Not before you finish tending to the fence. Several of those posts need replacing," Alma scolded, both hands on her hips.

Head lowered, I left the wheel behind and went back outside.

❧

As darkness fell and there was no more use being outdoors, the sisters ushered me back into the house.

"Not bad for a first day," Mina praised.

"Except for when Gilly tried to snap at you. That sheep is going to become a nice mutton stew if she keeps it up," Edna said, double checking my arm just to be sure I was unscathed.

"Let's see, we've covered sheep care, fence mending, stall repairing. Is there anything else?" Alma asked, counting the jobs on her fingers.

I couldn't have stopped myself if I wanted to. The words bubbled up from my soul, hot and eager. "Can I spin now?"

They gave me a wide-eyed look. "My goodness. We forgot the most important part!" Mina exclaimed. "Of course you can spin. What use is having sheep if you don't use their wool?"

Whisking me back up the ladder, we stood before the machine. Its wood glistened in the low flames.

This time, the sisters explained all the parts of the wheel...what this metal piece did, and what that rotating part wound. How to properly prepare the wool and hold it just right. *You must pinch the wool, if you care to know.* Bobbins, carding, drafting, all were among the hundreds of words they hurtled at me at such speed I was barely able to keep up. It didn't matter. I listened and learned, soaking it all up, storing it away to think over, review, and memorize later. Their lesson concluded on the floor brushing bits of wool, a basket still remaining to be carded.

"It's a shame yarn doesn't pay more for the work, but that's just part of the trade, I'm afraid," Alma said grabbing a new piece of wool, scratching the paddles over the springy white ball.

"Better one has a trade that makes some money than no trade at all," Mina replied.

"If only we could spin wool into gold," Edna said.

All three cackled at the idea.

"Now, before we set this boy mad with dreaming from our silly ideas, let's see how much he's learned," Mina said, standing and directing me to the wheel.

They gathered around as I set everything up just as they said. Placing the bobbin in the correct position, winding the wool just right. Then I treadled, and the wheel spun.

I heard clapping in the distance, but my mind was already too focused on the methodical pumping.

Whirr! Whirr! Whirr!

Funny, though, as I spun I couldn't help but imagine the fuzzy ball in my hand twisting into gold, shining brightly twirling around the bobbin.

I chuckled to myself at the very thought of it. Such an intriguing idea those sisters had. Too bad it was only fantasy.

THE YEARS PASSED, and every morning that I woke beneath the sisters' roof, I was grateful.

They had been my salvation, though they didn't realize to what extent. They did only what came natural to them, showing me affection in the form of hugs and sweet cakes. To repay their kindness, I always did my chores without protest. I fed the sheep just as the sun rose over the hills, carded their wool, and spun it into yarn. They had my absolute devotion. I even grew to enjoy their sisterly squabbles.

"The fork doesn't go on the right, it goes on the left, Edna!" Mina would correct, eyeing her closely as she set the table for dinner.

"I read in *Etiquette of His Royal Majesty* that the fork, in fact, goes on the right," Edna snapped back, placing the fork on the right with a loud bang of defiance.

"Technically," Alma would chime in, not ever wanting to be left out of an argument, "Forks are not traditionally used for Soufflé."

For the first time since the king had shattered my life, I was happy. I found this especially true when I would spin. I would feed it my fury, centering on the spiraling mouth of the bobbin as it feasted eagerly. Then, the gentle whirr of the wheel would lull and quell the hatred for the king. The animosity infecting my heart dissipated. I thought that maybe I could start again.

But, as usual, pain always found its way back to me.

Those rumors I heard long ago of the sisters using witchcraft were not completely untrue. Every night, the odd objects that had been stuck in nooks and crannies slowly emerged from hiding. Pendulums, crystals, stacks of cards, all sorts of fascinating items suddenly appeared. Alma added the final touch, covering the oil lamps on the wall with a purple cloth. The gold embroidered stars twinkled as the light illuminated them from behind.

Once Alma covered the final lamp I was given some sort of sweet, and sent up to my loft for the night. As the night deepened eager knocks rumbled the door.

In the beginning I thought nothing of it, perfectly content with my apple turnover or slice of cherry tart. However, sweets can only quell a boy's curiosity for so long.

Careful not to make a sound I tiptoed down my ladder, making sure to stand flat against the cool wall once my feet hit the bottom.

With solemn decorum, the sisters circled the crystal ball I had first seen when I arrived. Bowing, Mina removed the black velvet revealing the pure orb and lifted it up towards the sky. Edna and Alma burnt a bouquet of sage underneath, the pungent smoke traveling up the smooth glass.

Taking the hands of their customer, Alma and Edna would lead them to a seat at the table with the crystal in the middle. Mina sat motionless on the other side. The customer would ask her a question or confess a worry. Mina would look deep into the crystal, waving her hands over the clear surface, muttering something inaudible.

Mina's eyes remained closed as her hands hovered just above the round surface. They would then sit in absolute silence. After several long moments, Mina would open her eyes and she would speak, her words received with smiles, swears, grimaces, or even occasionally, sobs.

IT WAS MY FIFTEENTH BIRTHDAY.

As I sat in the chair by the fire, Edna and Alma dug a pendulum out of a flowerpot. Mina walked towards me as she had every night. But tonight, I noticed no cake in her hand.

"It is time," she said serenely.

"For what?" I asked as she kissed my forehead.

"Why, it is your fifteenth year!" Alma exclaimed stacking a pile of colorful, illustrated cards on the table. "A very important age. We have been waiting a long time for this day."

"Today you become a man, and it's only proper we see what fate has in store for you," Mina said, walking over to the crystal ball.

Edna swiftly covered the lamps and the light grew dim. Mina removed the black velvet cover revealing the flawless globe and motioned me to come.

I was thrilled to see the sphere again, this time even closer. My skin tingled with the sensation of falling through water.

"It has always been a great pity we couldn't read your future until now," Alma said. "But that's the thing with the future. It's very picky about when it will allow itself to be revealed."

"Yes, very improper to expose someone so young," Edna added.

"How does it work?" I asked, putting out my hand to touch the globe.

I was stopped by a tap on the wrist and cluck of a tongue.

"The crystal grants us the ability to decipher the phantoms contained within, illuminating the path one will take. It is an ancient art form designed to channel the energy around us to its fullest extent," Mina answered.

"We have often wondered what path fate has chosen for you," Edna said.

She grasped my hand with a squeeze and sat me down in the chair.

Alma gathered a bundle of sage from under the table and lit it. A plume of smoke rose from the smoldering leaves, and the scent filled my lungs.

Mina lifted the crystal above her head while Edna and Alma held the sage underneath, muttering words in a strange language. Once the ritual was complete, Mina laid the ball back onto its cushion. Her eyes glazed over as she stared into the realm of the orb.

"This will be your destiny, child. We hope it has many blessings in store for you," Alma and Edna whispered in my ears.

I beamed, hoping my future would be filled with the same joys I had known during these past years. Truly, I asked nothing more.

A serene feeling took me and icy water ran over my body as I stared into the clarity of the sphere. It wanted to know me, asking for my secrets, my dreams. Unable to resist, I told it everything.

Without warning, I found myself naked, submerged in a vast black ocean. There was quiet around me, my soul weightless as I swam fully exposed to the universe. I didn't want to leave this feeling of complete and pure liberation. However, the ocean began to shrink around me. First it dried into a pond, then a puddle until there was no water left at all and I only felt the hard back of my chair.

I shook my head and opened my eyes, curious to find out what was in store for me.

Mina's face was frozen in terror, and a similar rictus infected Alma and Edna.

"A...a Shadow!" Mina gasped.

Alma and Edna released my hands like they held the very plague. Confusion tore through me.

"My poor dear boy!" Alma cried out.

Edna clapped her hands to her mouth, stifling a cry.

"A deep darkness dwells in this boy, deceit and devastation lying in his wake," Mina pronounced. "Sisters, we have unwittingly allowed a Shadow to live beneath our roof."

They made several signs with their hands as if to protect them from an evil force—from...me.

"A Shadow?" I asked, every feeling of horror suspended by a single thread of truth that was ready to snap.

Mina answered, "A Shadow is a kind of being, feeding on our energy driven by its own purposes, no care of others capable of reaching its stale heart. These creatures are usually born from our hopelessness, nothing but a shade, a reflection of our darkest emotions. But never has there been a creature mingling both human and shadow as one. Until now. You boy, are destined for a dual spirit."

The sister's faces were ashen now. Blood rushed through my ears and fear ate into my stomach. I couldn't accept they actually believed this of me. It was just a stupid ball of glass.

"That's insane," I said, pretending a calm that was as worthless as a paper hat in a rainstorm. "You've practically raised me. Never once have I spoken an ill word or ever wanted to do harm. Now you are going to believe what some crystal tells you over what you know to be true?"

Even as I spoke, I looked into their eyes and knew. Their opinion would not change. In that moment, my heart and my life shattered beyond repair.

"Such ghastly images I saw! Straw, gold, a child. I have never received such a foul reading in all my years," Mina whispered, refusing to meet my gaze any longer.

"We never should have taken him in," Edna muttered.

"Now we know why we lost so much business. It was the darkness within him," Alma said coldly.

My hands rolled into fists and they pumped with the anger thundering in my soul.

"So that's it then?" I spat, jumping to my feet. "I'm just supposed to accept that I'm some vile creature intent on destruction?"

"We told you we believed in fate, and fate has marked you, my poor one. There is nothing to be done. You cannot un-write what is written," Mina replied, her voice as grim as the grave.

I stared at them, hot tears running down my cheeks, willing them to reconsider. This was utter lunacy! Couldn't they see that? No, they couldn't. They were too afraid of me now. Afraid of what I was destined to be.

They turned away from me, and once again I was that outcast little boy, shivering outside in the cold.

"You must leave us. Tonight," Mina said, facing the wall. "We cannot allow you to stay. You have darkened our door far too long."

The others remained silent, and I bit my lip in angry disbelief at their betrayal.

A bodiless hand gripped my heart, its fist squeezing out all the ice until all that remained within was flames. The pain I thought gone returned. But this time, it was deeper, etching itself within my flesh and soul, encompassing everything until I felt nothing else.

I saw the crystal sitting brazenly there, mocking me for having ever believed I could move on. For having believed I could trust another person.

Without a second thought I picked it up and threw it against the floor. A loud crack echoed through the room as the glass exploded around my feet. Bits of crystal flew all over, the ball destroyed into a million pieces just as my soul.

"See," I heard Alma whisper. "It has already taken hold."

She might as well have stuck a knife in my chest and carved out my living heart.

Willing my breaths to slow, I observed the results of my destruction. The women cowered in my presence, but I no longer felt a part of their world. It was like I was a giant, looking down on some other race below. Small and weak. Silly.

My quarrel wasn't with them. They were the victims of inane superstition, of the reputation that never really stopped haunting me. They hadn't made me the outcast.

The king had.

He had thrown me into this abyss when he destroyed everything I loved. He made me this thing. This Shadow. For the first time, I saw clearly what I must do.

The king must pay for his sins.

I would take back what was taken from me, my name and family avenged. Only then would the pain woven into my bones finally be unraveled. In that moment, my revenge was born. I would show them all they were wrong. When the king paid for the sins he committed against his subjects, they would thank me.

They all would thank me.

CHAPTER FOUR

THE THIRD DAY: LAILA

"**Remember," the stranger** said before he vanished with the dawn. "Pain is power."

Then he was gone, and I was left alone with enough gold to buy the whole world.

Glistening spools were stacked in whimsical towers that swayed from their impressive height. Some of the stacks resembled castle walls and pillars, and others the shape of crumbling ruins. I touched the smooth, metallic twine, and its lifeless chill sunk into my fingers. To me, the golden walls were nothing more than a dungeon. I was the gold's prisoner, each thin thread as unbreakable as an iron bar.

But not for much longer.

I heard the telltale protesting squeal of the door and the sound of footsteps on the stairs. A figure emerged from the gleaming haze of the gold, and I knew the time had come.

King Edward moved towards me, running his fingers over his lips. The look of utter amazement on his face as he surveyed his glittering prize disgusted me as usual. But, I found myself paying attention to the strength and handsomeness of his features. It left me unsettled, but nothing would sway me from my course.

"In two short nights you have made me richer than any monarch of any kingdom in the whole of history," he said, inspecting the heavy spool he now held.

"Then your majesty is satisfied with what I have provided?" I asked, morbid curiosity pushing me to make him reveal just what exactly he had planned for me. Not that I planned on being surprised.

"Nearly. I believe I have almost all I need," he answered in a preoccupied tone. Thankfully, his new riches distracted him from noticing my hands ball into fists. I hated that I had guessed correctly.

"You wish me to spin again?"

"Of course! One more night, at least for now. Yes, one more night should be quite sufficient for the time being."

As if I believed him. Men like him would never be satisfied.

"After I have spun your gold for another night, what will you do with me?" I asked, growing impatient for him to reveal his plans so I could put my own into play.

Putting down the spool he focused his gaze on me, like a wolf eyeing some spectacularly talented hare. "Keep you somewhere safe."

"Safe? Where would this 'safe' place be, your majesty?"

He let out a frustrated sigh. "Stop thinking of yourself for a moment and consider the broader issues your very existence creates. If my enemies ever discovered the source of my wealth, there would be war for sure. Entire nations would rise up to fight for such an asset. Do you really want to be responsible for such bloodshed?"

"So I am to remain locked away until you have brought war to all other nations and vanquished their threat?" I snapped.

He chuckled and grasped my shoulders. "I would wager anything I provide is far nicer than that hellhole you came from. Why would you even want freedom if it meant being chained to a drunk? The best prospect you could ever hope to have would be a marriage to some farm boy who prefers the comfort of a sheep over a woman."

I let the bite of his words fill me and fuel my pain...and my power. For the first time, he was right, which was all the more reason to bend him to my will.

"That's where you are wrong, your majesty," I said, looking him squarely in the eye. "You are assuming I want my freedom. I don't."

His condescending satisfaction disappeared into confusion. His fingers dug into my shoulders.

"I don't understand," he said. "Isn't that what this little interrogation is about? Trying to weasel your way to go home to your felonious father?"

"That man can burn in hell," I shot back. "I am no longer concerned about him, or with anyone for that matter. I only have concern for myself."

His eyes narrowed, and I was surprised he didn't command me to quit my insolence. Not that I would have listened at this point. I realized the real truth of the stranger's words. My pain had cost me everything, but now, with nothing to lose, I had everything to gain.

"I have now spun more gold for you than all other kingdoms combined," I said matter-of-factly. My hands trembled, but thankfully, my voice didn't. "I think I deserve a reward for my efforts."

"You mean your head is not reward enough?" he chuckled. "My, someone imagines they have the right to bargain with her king."

Blood pounded in my ears and pumped power through my veins.

"No. It is you who are mistaken if you think you have the right to bargain with *me*," I retorted, the bite of my words extinguishing his amusement. "We both know you don't dare kill me. I am far too valuable, as you just admitted moments ago. You won't risk the chance of losing the only thing standing between you and endless wealth."

"You ungrateful bitch!" he seethed.

"In fact," I continued, loving the taste of strength on my tongue. "You should consider the greater game at play now. You won't kill me, but that doesn't mean I won't kill myself. It wouldn't be difficult to do, and all of the gold I have ever spun will turn to ash just as my corpse."

His cheeks engorged with blood and his fists shook. "You lie. You wouldn't do such a thing," he hissed.

"Are you willing to take that chance? To test me? I am not afraid of death."

He considered my words for several long moments. Slowly, his anger dissolved into a disturbing calm.

"For a peasant you are quite cunning," he said with forced civility. "If you don't want to be free, what is it you want?"

I gave him my sweetest smile and said, "I want to be queen."

He looked as if I had punched him in the gut.

"I will spin for you for one more night," I continued. "Then, you can never ask me to spin again. You will make me your queen, and you will never have to fear that I shall fall prey to another kingdom or that your wealth will turn to ash."

He looked at me hard and crossed his arms. My breathing remained steady and my gaze firm. I would not let this opportunity pass by without a fight. The king might have been a merciless ogre, but he wasn't stupid.

"You make a compelling argument, one I see I have no choice but to accept," he said finally, his tone flat and blunt. "My gold means more to me than anything, and I refuse to let it be lost. You want to be queen? Very well. We are agreed. You will be my wife and my queen, and I will keep the gold you have spun for me."

A long breath slowly escaped through my lips. Elation bubbled up in my heart. For the first time in my life, I was the maker of my own fate, and what a fate it was to be!

He studied me, his expression shifting, then said, "In truth, there would be no other noble bride who could bring such a dowry as the one you have spun for me. The more I think on it, this is actually a blessing."

King Edward picked up a lock of my hair and held it to his face, inhaling the scent of the expensive rose and citrus oils still lingering in the strands. A flush of heat rolled through my veins as I realized the price I must pay for the life I desired.

"Exquisite," he murmured, "I see now how great a shame it would have been to lock away something so uncommonly beautiful as yourself. Let it not be said that it is only riches that I seek, for I will appreciate all that is lovely and good. In fact, you might present an added benefit to this union you desire. I have yearned for an heir for quite some time, and with those wide hips of yours and hearty peasant stock, I think you should do the job nicely. No more noble stillborn weaklings for me."

He placed his finger beneath my chin and brought my lips to meet his own. I should have been repulsed and full of righteous disgust as his lips brushed mine. But only triumph filled my heart. He was nothing but a prize I had won, just as I was his prize. He might have enjoyed the benefit of lust as well, but I was the one with the power. Even though after tonight I would never spin gold again, I would present the kingdom with the greatest treasure of all, one that would render my position and future unassailable. I would give the kingdom an heir. My son would save me as no grown man ever would.

"Come," he said, breaking our kiss, and so lost was I in my thoughts that I had almost forgotten I was being kissed. "Why don't you rest before this final night of spinning? I dare say, if I am only to get one more night out of you, I need to make the most of it. Let's see just how much gold you can spin with these lovely fingers of yours."

Taking my hand and kissing each fingertip, he led me back up the stairs, calling servants to start bringing down as much straw as they could find. He wanted the spinning room filled to bursting.

A forest of dry twigs was all that separated me now from becoming queen. Only one more night with the stranger, and everything I wanted would come to pass.

THE THIRD DAY: RUMPELSTILTSKIN

Tonight, everything rested on one word.

I lay on my back, listening to the rain grow louder. Flashes of lightning made the cracks in the plaster walls crawl. Even the timber of the building trembled in fear with each growl of the storm.

A clap of thunder reverberated throughout my body, awakening my need for the chaos Laila promised. I didn't have to doubt for a moment the king would request more from her, and I was eager to see if the bitch would bite the hand that fed her straw.

I inhaled, searching the scents for the smallest trace of desperation. Thunder rumbled again, and I breathed in, inviting the grief of the entire kingdom to enter me, hunting for my prey. It would not be pleasant, but these things rarely were.

The air inside my lungs shifted, expanding until the threads of sounds that were trapped within it unwound and sang like the strings of a violin. At first it was one heartbeat, then two, then a thousand. Every beat full of wailing and crying, begging. The roar filled my ears with such intensity I feared my head would crack open like a fractured egg, the yolk of humanity's sins and grief running out as viscous as it was vicious.

I persevered, searching through them for the one I desired.

Gradually the other sounds dissipated, leaving only one that caused a flush of heat to ripple across my skin. A singular and fluid thump. A heart, but not just any old lump of flesh. This heart was Laila's.

The pulse grew more distinct, and I relished the beautiful fusion of anxiety and terror driving every beat.

Summoning myself towards that delicious sound, forms took shape around me. *Pop!* There appeared a spinning wheel. *Pop!* A pile of empty spools materialized beside a wall. *Whoosh!* The ceiling arched high over my head, and pillars burst through the stone floor, taking their place in the room that became more solid around me by the second.

I stood staring in utter astonishment, surrounded by the purest greed I'd ever witnessed. The previous two rooms were nothing matched to this. Sandcastles compared to great, proud towers. Straw rolled in avalanches across the treacherous landscape, like snow from the highest mountains come to crush all before it. Tonight, however, showed a man determined never to have want of gold again. If only he knew how each twig of straw I touched spun him tighter into the web of fate I wove.

Laila stood tall with a dress of red silk fanning like flames around her. This was no longer the whiny little peasant girl I first encountered. This was a woman with a spirit to be reckoned with.

I already congratulated myself on this triumph though she had spoken no words, as the king would not dress anyone in such a manner unless she was well worth the expense. Though I had created her for him, I couldn't stop twisting my mouth at the thought of him running those grubby hands of his down something so fine. Laila was no more than a pawn, a throwaway piece, but she was *my* pawn. Yes, I had sacrificed her like any good strategist would to secure my larger game, yet this small victory for the king rankled me.

"How did it feel?" I asked smoothly, disciplining my thoughts back to the moment.

I enjoyed her start of surprise as she whirled around to face me. A delightful haughtiness emanated from her, though not enough to hide that delectable flame of desperation in her soul. I could sense it smoldering.

"How did what feel?" she asked.

"Bringing a king to his knees, of course!" I chuckled as I walked over to her. "Or was it your knees you fell to in order to get that regal gown of yours?"

With exquisite delicacy, I picked a minute piece of straw from the neckline of her gown, my fingers never once coming in contact with her skin. She shuddered though her eyes burned.

"I did no such thing," she said, then tossed her head back proudly. "I had no *need* to do any such thing.

"Of course you didn't. So you took my advice?"

She stared at me and then a dark, deep smile slowly curved her lips, causing her entire face to shine with a beautiful malice. She took my breath away, and I was lost in admiration for this newly born monster standing before me.

"Tell me, what did you decide to make your puppet do?" I asked, shaking off the spell of her smile.

Pure satisfaction glowed on her features as she walked to the spinning wheel and gave it a good whirl.

"I told him I would only spin for one more night, and after, he will make me his queen."

I grabbed the wheel and abruptly stopped it from spinning. Seeing her touch the wheel felt as if she was touching me in some deeply invasive, intimate way. It was wrong. I was the one who controlled the wheel, who made it turn, not her. Yet, the vicious giggle that fell from her lips made me want to both hear it again and silence it—preferably with my own lips.

"You are quite the vixen!" I said, moving so close to her I felt the heat of her hate. "Then, all that needs to be done is for me to spin this entire room into gold so you can grasp that devilish dream in your hot fingers. By now you know how this works. What do you intend to pay me to claim this great victory of yours?"

The flame in her soul burned hotter. She tried to spin the wheel again, but I was quicker and slapped my hand down to stop it. I tutted indignantly. No matter how clever my girl was, a novice may not teach the master.

"Once I am queen I can offer you payment in any form you wish.

Land, wealth, titles. Name it and it will be yours."

"What use would I have with those?" I asked.

"I don't understand! You only wanted a necklace and a bit of worthless silver before. What I'm offering is far more valuable than anything I've given you yet."

I chuckled. A pawn playing a queen is still just a pawn. Every move she made would be dictated by me until I said otherwise.

Her desperation raged now like an inferno, consuming her soul, and for the first time, I felt a frisson of danger. Fire was a mindless element, but it destroyed all the more because of it. I reminded myself that even a pawn can become a queen when played right, and then, she will be commanded by none. Laila would be a burning queen.

"I already spin straw into gold, so I have no need of money or jewels," I explained patiently, as if to a particularly stupid child. "I don't wish for a title. The aristocracy is quite dull. All that yammering about bloodlines and ancestors. It's enough to put me to sleep just thinking about it. No, my dear miller's daughter, you will have to be much more creative in thinking up a reward for me. I suggest you think on your feet, as the night is moving on and time waits for no one." Except me, but now was not the time to go into that.

She stared at me, her lips pursed in a quivering moue. "I've come too far to lose everything now."

"That is hardly my problem."

"You made it your problem when you saved me that first night!"

"Not at all. That was a one-time business transaction. I never offer anything on a subscription basis."

I could see in her eyes she was but half-a-heartbeat from slapping me. I closed the distance between us, using my height to tower over her. She glared back at me, and I saw in the dark depths of her eyes a glint of obsidian, forged in the fires of her desperation, glass made steel from hate and need. I wanted to kiss her eyes.

No! I did not. She spoke as I struggled to contain my wayward thoughts.

"You think I am a fool," she said. "But, I know that you would not be here if I did not yet have something you wanted. So, cease to play the fool yourself and tell me!"

She panted in her rage, her stays straining with each deep breath, lifting her breasts almost obscenely, as if to taunt me.

"The night," she said, imitating my tone perfectly, "is moving on, and time waits for no one."

I was undone by her taunting, tragic smile.

I slid my hand over her left breast, sliding my fingers under the clinging neckline of her gown to grasp her and center my palm on her heartbeat.

Hungering for her flesh and despair, I gave in and opened the floodgates to sensation. Pain. Passion. Pleasure. Perjury. Pleading. Each beat of her heart screamed at me, blasting my self back like the heat of the furnace. I fought to stay within her, pushing with all my strength, locking my lust and my need into her like talons into tissue. Ah, there it was. Pride. Dear old Pride rose up within her soul and fought me off like a she-lion, tearing my claws from her, no matter the injury to herself.

Yet, of all the things that made me need her in that moment, it was Pride that aroused me the most. Pride was prickly and capricious, yet curiously forthright. With Pride, Laila became fierce, knocking my hand off her breast.

It was my pride, or perhaps my own despair, that had me grasping her face and attacking her lips with mine. She bit me, and I bit back. She snarled and grabbed my hair, yanking hard. I slammed her into the wall of straw. She dug her nails into my jaw, suddenly pulling me toward her instead of pushing away. I seized her hips and ground myself into her.

"Is this what you want?" she panted as I sucked at the pulse point of her throat, as if I could draw the venom of Pride from her. "I'll give it to you if this is your price!"

Blackness closed in on me.

When I opened my eyes, I was across the room from her, and she was on the ground where I had thrown her down. I stared at her, watching her gasping and struggling to right herself, her dress, her hair. She bore the marks of my lips on her skin like bruises on silk.

I berated myself silently, though I was oddly devoid of feeling. I searched my senses for disgust at her or revulsion at my weakness. Had the look in her eyes been anything but vulnerable confusion, I might have found the anger to taunt her. As it was, I had nothing except the flatness of my eternal purpose.

"I...am willing," Laila whispered. "It wouldn't be...just...just for the price."

I strained to resist the call of the fraught fruit of her soul. I took a deep breath and exhaled slowly, clearing the smoke of lust from my lungs.

"That is not my price," I said. I opened my mouth to sneer at her, but I had no words, and her words did not bear considering for all the temptation they suddenly held.

"Your first-born child," I blurted out. I had intended to give a grandiose, teasing speech about the king's greed, but apparently, this was the best I could manage in the moment.

Laila's glare turned poisonous. I braced to fight my she-lion once more.

"My child? Are you serious?" she asked in a low tone.

"The question isn't if I'm serious," I smirked, recovering my composure some. "The question is, are you? Your child is my price. Either you want your precious royal title, or you want to be the hero to an imaginary child and die a martyr."

I was impatient for her reply, ready now with quick rebuttals to the impassioned, "Anything but that!" or the even more melodramatic, "I'd rather die!"

"All right. I agree,"

"You are awfully calm about such a decision," I snapped to cover my confusion. "I thought motherhood was the greatest gift for a woman?"

"I don't want the king's brat," she spat. "I know all too well what it is to be raised by the cruel and uninterested. No, if I do bear a child for the king, it would be a mercy to take it far away from us."

"Whatever helps you sleep at night," I said, ignoring the lump of icy foreboding in the pit of my stomach.

I flicked my wrist with a flourish. A fresh roll of parchment appeared in my hand, its words ready to bind her to me forever.

THE THIRD DAY: LAILA

H**e gave me** a deep, courtly bow. With a mocking smile on those same lips that had devoured me only moments earlier, he handed me a scroll.

"What's this?" I asked stupidly.

He rolled his eyes and gestured for me to unfurl it.

How I hated him!

I hated that he could burn me down to ash and rebuild me in his image. I hated he gave me power. I hated that I now understood how deep his pain must be in order for him to be so powerful. I hated that I had offered myself in power, and that his pain had refused me.

The edge of the scroll fell to my feet, rolling out across the floor and revealing thousands of tiny words scribbled.

"It's a contract," he said blithely. "Nothing too complicated, I assure you. I like arrangements such as ours to be neat and tidy. Don't want any misunderstandings later."

A black quill materialized between his fingers, the smooth fibers of the feather glistening in the torchlight. He held it out to me, laid out across his palm. Running perpendicular to it was a scar that jaggedly ran from finger to wrist.

Without thinking, I brushed the feather to the floor and grasped his hand in mine, pulling it closer to study the fierce scar. It looked fresh, and the thin layer of new skin over seemed to seal in a chasm of turbulent, swirling black blood underneath.

"I've never seen such a scar," I said, tracing it with the tip of my finger.

He stared down at his hand. "An accident when I was much younger. Are you quite through? There is a room full of straw to spin."

I paused, listening to the humming of the blood in my veins. Power. Pain.

"It was the result of someone teaching me a lesson," he ground out.

"What lesson?" I asked, keeping my voice low.

Like a snake striking, he coiled his fingers around my wrist and yanked me against him.

"That what we want the most always has a price," he spat, glaring into my eyes as his jaw clenched and pulsed. "Time is ticking. Make your choice. Your neck or your child?"

He forced the quill into my hand and stalked away. I stared squarely at the empty space waiting for my name. Only a few drops of ink and everything I wanted would be mine.

I stopped, the tip of the quill just above the paper. His blatant eagerness feeding a newfound fear. My heart was cold, but it wasn't vile. What if I was damning this unborn child to a fate worse than being raised by the king? I couldn't abandon a child to an unknown fate.

"Is there a problem?" he asked.

"Promise me," I said, the quill still hovering over the page. "You will not harm this child. That you will protect it at all costs and give it a happy life. Make it an addendum to this contract or else, I won't sign."

He scowled, his features hardening into a frightening mask as he came back to stand before me, looming tall and full of menace.

"You are in no position to bargain, you neophyte. I will not be twisted into acquiescing to your whims," he hissed.

"I'm not a fool. You are too keen for this child. It is important to you, isn't it?"

A flicker of surprise shone in his eyes, but he quickly doused it in cold aloofness.

"It is! I see now!" I exclaimed. "You hate the king just as much as I do. You want to break him, and this child allows you leverage of some sort."

He bared his teeth and grabbed both my arms.

"That's my business," he seethed. "Mind your own."

"My business is the safety of myself and this child. Do you really want an innocent to suffer? To know the poisonous pain we both have thriving in our hearts? Surely not."

The storms in his eyes stilled, though his expression remained stony. Releasing me he paced back and forth, running his fingers over his mouth and chin. After a moment, he reached a decision and waved a hand over the parchment. Several new lines appeared.

"The child shall encounter no harm," he said bluntly. "Satisfied now?"

"Yes," I replied, my heart a fraction more at ease. I positioned the quill properly in my fingers.

"The inkpot?" I asked, expecting him to produce it out of thin air as he had the quill and scroll.

He just glared and pointed at the quill. I shrugged in reply. If he wasn't concerned about ink, then I wasn't either. Perhaps the ink was magical or invisible.

I pulled the quill along the parchment. A burning sting crept along under the skin of my fingers. It was mild at first, but with each letter, the pain grew until I felt like my hands were full of fire. Only once I finished the final letters of my name did I realize the source of the discomfort.

My name was written in my own blood.

"I forgot to mention that bit. Only blood will do, I'm afraid," he said, his lips curled with an odd satisfaction.

Taking the quill and the contract from me he scribbled his own name below my own. I couldn't make out a single letter of his childish-looking handwriting. His hand shook as the tip scratched across the page, letting out a small hiss as he finished with a big flourish. Evidently, he was required to sign in blood as well. Rolling up the contract, he grasped both it and the quill tightly in his hand. Without a sound, both blinked into nothingness.

"Now that we have wasted a sufficient amount of time placating your majesty's whims, I suggest we get started. I would hate to leave this unfinished because someone couldn't leave well enough alone," he sneered.

I picked up a basket full of straw, shoving it at his chest with the sweetest, most deadly smile I could manage.

A mountain range of golden twigs waited to be brought to his feet. I grabbed armfuls of straw, wincing with every sharp poke or bite, but I no longer cared. Each one served as a reminder I would never have to endure such suffering again.

The whir of the wheel filled the silence that descended upon us.

Back and forth I trudged. Baskets filled, and baskets emptied. All the time he sat spinning, tossing the spools behind him, a loud crack vibrating through the stone as they smacked together in their landing.

I cursed the maid for having thought silk an appropriate fabric for such labor. Sweat broke across my forehead and between my breasts. Heat consumed me. Unable to bear it anymore, I peeled the wet fabric from my body, leaving the accursed gown in a heap on the floor. Thankfully, my linen chemise allowed a small respite from the heat, and I could keep up with the rhythm that the spinning wheel and its master demanded.

Crack.

I couldn't help but sneak a few brief moments to watch him spin. There was a frightening delicacy about the way he did it. He firmly gripped the straw, twisting the twigs between his fingers and palms. He caressed the ropes of straw. Loved them. Stroked them as if they were the body of a woman.

I hated the straw. I wanted to be the straw. I wanted him to spin me, twist me, transform me. I burned with the memory of his fingers on the skin of my breast, and I licked my lips to taste the blood from our biting kisses. He had given me power from my pain. Did he know that he had taught me that pain could also be pleasure?

A thump at my feet startled me from my randy reverie, and I saw that I had dropped my basket.

"Don't tell me you've already worn yourself out," he mocked from the wheel. "I thought you were used to hard work, or do you usually work best on your back?"

That man was an arrogant, hateful bastard. There was a moment when he was in very great danger of having me chuck a golden bobbin or three at his skull. Instead, I huffed, picked up my basket, and went back to work.

THE THIRD DAY: RUMPELSTILTSKIN

I **relished every** exquisite letter. The smoky despair in each drop of blood on the parchment promised me eternity.

Laila was bound to me forever.

However, my self-congratulations were overshadowed by the fact that I, too, had signed in blood. My own. No one ever dared demand such a thing with me. Perhaps they had never thought of it. But Laila was a quick study and brazen enough to turn the tables on her teacher. Oh, yes, she would be a great queen...until I brought fate crashing down upon her head.

I swallowed a roll of regret. It was distasteful to be the agent of her destruction. I refused to dwell on it. It was easier to accept regretting that these evenings were at an end.

Perhaps it was not such a bad thing. The way she strutted around in nothing but a thin chemise had my cock hard and angry. Every curve was on display as the fabric clung to the sweat dripping down her back and over her thighs. I wanted to peel that chemise off her. With my teeth.

"You are going to break the spinning wheel if you keep up that speed," she remarked.

I started and saw the wheel was rocking, creaking and groaning. A cramp started to coil in my leg. I hadn't realized how quickly I was peddling. Rage thundered through me at having allowed myself to be distracted and by such a thing as...as...a woman. No, worse. By such a thing as Laila.

"I didn't realize you were such an expert on spinning, seeing as you need me to do it," I snapped.

"You are odious," she grumbled, plopping down a freshly filled basket.

That garden of blushes blossomed over her chest again and I couldn't help but notice her breasts rising and falling with each breath. The sweat beading atop them glistened in the torchlight. On the morrow, they would become property of the king. He would put his hands on them. He would put his mouth to them. It would be *his* name that she cried aloud, not mine. Never would be mine, for my name was forever forbidden. All logic was lost to me.

"I rather be odious than the king's whore," I shot back.

What was wrong with me? I saw her tremble in anger from the corner of my eye. I had done it.

"More insults!" she shouted. "Fine. Ignore me," she spat. "But I will not stand for it anymore, you hear?"

"Or what?" I seethed, jumping to my feet, knocking the spinning wheel over, frothy tangles of gold spewing from the wheel.

I walked towards her, forcing her back against the stone wall now that there was not straw to block it. I blocked her in, my hands on either side of her head, palms flat against the cold rock. She smelled of roses and salt.

"What could you possibly do?" I continued, "You prance around thinking you are master of your own fate. You know nothing of fate, what fate really is. Fate is a wild card. It chooses favorites and you are simply damn fortunate it chose you. Well, for now, anyway. That's the thing with fate. It changes just as quickly as luck."

She gave a deep, throaty laugh and said, "You're mad."

I grabbed her arms. Her flesh was soft as it gave beneath my grip.

"Of course you'd think that. Anything that is not within your pathetic realm of comprehension is automatically thought of as mad,"

I hissed, pulling her closer, feeling the soft bends and arcs of her body against mine. "I've lived things you've only seen in your nightmares."

Our gazes burned into one another's. Her lips parted as if to speak, but only silence came out of them. We didn't move, didn't even breathe.

Her gaze grew heavy and dark. I loosened my grip, letting one hand slide around her waist, while the other dug into her hair. If it was madness she wanted from me, then madness I would give her. She lifted her chin, and I claimed her mouth.

The curves of her lips pulsed with blood and desire. Unable to stop, I grazed my teeth over their supple flesh, delicate and hot, and knew she was my salvation.

I stilled.

Salvation? I didn't want salvation.

I pulled away, leaving her looking confused. For the first time I saw her for what she was. She was a siren leading me towards my own defeat, and I was the fool willingly sailing towards her.

Her spell on me was broken. I tugged my shirt straight, ignoring her as she tucked a lock of her disheveled hair behind her ear.

"There are still baskets left needing to be spun," I said.

Any expression she wore before melted away into a blank mask.

"I'll go get them," she replied. Picking up a basket, she moved quicker than ever, staying as far away from me as she could.

Running hot fingers through my hair, I sat down at the wheel, grinding my teeth at the pulsing discomfort between my legs. My body was fighting me, and my mind was proving to be a weaker warrior than I expected. Picking up a handful of dry twigs, I shook the lingering heat away and started to spin.

It was only a passing fancy. A moment of madness. Laila was a means to an end and that was all.

I spun in silence, and we spoke no more.

CHAPTER FIVE

Needle:

noun: a very fine slender piece of metal with a point at one end and a hole or eye for thread at the other, used in sewing.

verb: provoke or annoy (someone), especially by continual criticism or questioning.

THE LONG DEAD PAST: REBORN

After the Pythin Sisters' betrayal, I became again an endless wanderer, nothing but a silhouette against the night sky carrying a heart heavy with vengeance.

As much as I wanted to kill the king, it was easier said than done. He was untouchable within his castle walls and guards always at his side. Without proper planning, vengeance would be nothing short of suicide. I couldn't and wouldn't give him the pleasure of my blood, not when he had already taken my name.

Needless to say, I was at a loss how to exact my revenge.

Frustrated but still cautious, I had to keep to the outskirts of the cities I visited. I lived with the other outcasts beyond the walls that wanted to forget our existence. Drifters, actors, and prostitutes all became my unwilling family, and together we preyed upon those good citizens who dared to travel beyond the wall's safety and into our no-man's land.

I watched in fascination as my fellow frauds manipulated the crowd with unbelievable skill. Slickly spun superstition sold their snake oils and magical elixirs for them, devoted customers fervently purchasing their empty promises. At first, I felt sorry for the poor fools, but night after night as I watched them pay for a bit of rainwater in a shiny bottle, I realized I shouldn't pity fools because they were born never to know better. Besides, I was out of money, and my empty stomach grumbled with hunger. If their minds were too weak to see the truth in what I sold, why should I care?

I had never received so many gold coins in all my life, selling nothing but twigs, twine, and stones as protective runes against evil. Who knew the gullible afforded such wealth? I enjoyed the bewildered looks I inspired as I muttered incantations over the trinkets.

However, with the arrival of the gypsies one spring morning, fate indicated it had other plans than letting me fritter away my time fooling the foolish.

I marveled at how quickly their tents blossomed across the muddy field in a web of color. Once night fell, the real magic awoke when the tents glowed like colored paper lanterns in a carnival. Wild, wailing music rose from the campsite, a crazed mixture of drums and violins locked in a savage dance.

I had never seen anything quite like it before. A bearded woman spewed fire out of her mouth. A young man covered in tattoos created a stir by swallowing a curved sword—couldn't have been comfortable. Onlookers cheered at these oddities, throwing coins and hooting in amazed disbelief.

I milled at the back of a large crowd gathered around a small stage. They crammed themselves as tight as they could, standing on toes and peering over hats. The anticipation was palpable. Glancing up at the banner, I immediately understood the reason.

Red letters announced: *The Living Corpse*

Applause exploded around me. A hooded figure walked onto the wooden planks of the stage. Perhaps, not so much walked as *glided.*

A gangly, spidery man accompanied him, wearing tight black and yellow striped pants and a thick layer of white powder cracking in the creases on his forehead. He sported red paint on his cheeks, and a ridiculously thin black mustache.

He placed a finger against his lips, demanding silence.

"Ladies and gentlemen! What you are about to witness is not for the faint of heart. I *implore* those of weak disposition turn away now, lest your memories be haunted *forevermore*," he warned in a melodramatically ominous tone.

With such a tempting warning, the man guaranteed no one would refuse to open the Pandora's box he presented. Impatient grumbles rose from the audience, demanding to be shown what they came to see.

"You have made your choice! Prepare yourselves for the greatest mystery ever known, that of *The Living Corpse*!"

He grinned wickedly as he stepped back from the hooded figure, presenting him with an outstretched arm.

The figure threw off the cloak. Loud gasps rose up from the crowd. Several fainted while the rest looked visibly ill.

Upon the stage stood what was supposed to be a man, but he was only a monstrosity. He was not a dead thing as he should have been, but a living skeleton wrapped in cracking leathery skin. Yellow flesh hung from bony shoulders and hugged every ridge of his ribcage. There was no muscle or fat. There was only horror.

But all this paled to compare to his face. I beheld a skull covered in withered flesh, and where a nose should have been, was nothing but a black hole. His lips receded from his mouth in a ghastly grin, leaving behind a set of rotting teeth that grinned eternally.

What disturbed me the most were his eyes. They were perfectly shaped and a vibrant blue, all the life missing from his body shining through those two flawless orbs.

He seemed to enjoy the fear he inspired as he sauntered across the stage, sickly skin slinking over protruding bone with each step. His eyes searched the crowd, growing brighter anytime he heard a scream or cry.

He stopped. Extending a skeletal arm, he pointed down at a young woman. She trembled.

"Would you mind if I borrow your shawl?" he asked with impeccable politeness. "As you can imagine, I get rather chilly being just skin and bone." He made his teeth chatter, their mechanical toy-like movement causing nervous laughter to bubble and froth. Unable to refuse, she unwrapped her red shawl and placed it in his bony hand.

He took a few steps back, twisting the shawl between his fingers.

He released the fabric, but instead of falling to the ground, it stayed suspended in the air.

"Well, that's not all that amazing, is it?" he drawled as the audience clapped and hooted, demanding further astonishment.

He snapped his fingers and the floating shawl turned into a violin, a bow resting on top and waiting for its master's command.

"That is far more interesting!" he exclaimed. He paused briefly, then slowly moved his hands in long back and forth strokes, mimicking playing the violin.

The enchanted violin mirrored his movements, the most hauntingly beautiful sound emerging from its strings. The melody wrapped my soul in warmth, and my body swayed with every lilt and crescendo. For a moment, I believed I was floating just as the violin, weightless and pure.

But when he waved his hand and the music stopped, I felt my soul had been ripped from me. He snapped his fingers and the violin splintered until thousands of flakes of wood fell like snow onto the stage.

He rifled through the wood and retrieved a wad of red fabric. It was the woman's shawl, completely restored. Handing it back to her, he bowed, accepting the thunderous applause, the audience hailing him as some sort of horrific god. Enshrouding his body in the hooded robe, he descended from the stage, the crowd continuing their terrified praise, throwing gold coins onto the platform.

I was chilled.

Shaken.

I had never witnessed any magician perform such awesome feats. There were no strings, no detectable illusions or tricks. Many a charlatan had crossed my path, but never one so exquisitely skilled. So entranced, I barely noticed the spiderlike fingers creeping along my shoulder until the cold flesh brushed my neck. I spun around, facing the man with the mustache standing behind me. Up close, he looked as if he was the corpse, decaying with the powder melting from his oily skin.

"If you would follow me, sir," he said. "My master would like a word."

"Your master?" I asked, raising an eyebrow.

"*The Living Corpse*! I assure you, it is a great honor. He rarely speaks to outsiders." He laid his sweaty palm against my cheek and turned my head to the side as if inspecting me. "But something about you has garnered his particular... *interest*." He dramatically pronounced each syllable, ending with a snake-like hiss.

I shook him off, disgust driving the bile up from my stomach. "I'm not one of your freaks," I snarled. "What's all this nonsense about?"

"Apologies!" he exclaimed. "You must forgive me. It's just I've never seen such a divinely pale complexion."

I glared at him and an awkward silence swelled between us, until he cleared his throat, continuing. "My master thought you might need some coaxing, and wanted me to give you a message, if that be the case."

"And what message would that be?" I ground out the words against my will.

He lowered his chin and his eyes darkened. That pencil thin mustache curled with his menacing simper.

"That he can give you what you most desire."

LANTERNS FLICKERED as he led me with a quick step through the maze of tents. Shadows moving and shifting within the array of colored fabrics. Beside me, the figure of a woman undressed. Two men puffed rolls of smoke from cigars sitting at a table. Every life was on display to the world, any hope of secrets betrayed by light and shadow.

The odd man quickened his pace as we approached a tent on the far end of the camp. It glowed a deep red like a gem burning from within. He pulled back the thick fabric, waving me inside. The stiflingly heavy scent of incense burned and choked me.

Rubies and gold. Those were my first thoughts once I could breathe and see through the haze. I was in a bloody world bathed in golden light. Red Turkey carpets and mustard velvet cushions lay lazily about. In the center of the room was the Living Corpse himself, still shrouded in complete black.

"Here he is, master. Just as you requested." The man bowed with an obsequious flourish.

The Living Corpse exposed his skeletal hands and pulled down the hood uncovering his face. Ice and sweat broke out over my body at seeing his nightmarish disfigurement so close.

"Very good. You may go." His breath whistled through his crooked teeth as he waved the man away.

His vivid, blue eyes stared at me. Stared through me. I wanted to look away from his burning gaze, but I found I couldn't. Fear and morbid fascination made me immobile.

Desire seemed to emanate from him as he slunk slowly towards me. My body screamed to step back, to run.

"I've been waiting a long time for you," he finally said. "Ages, in fact!"

"For me?" I mastered the shaking in my voice and continued. After all, I reminded myself, we were but speaking charlatan-to-charlatan. "You must have me mistaken for someone else. I don't believe we've ever met. I do think I'd remember you."

He laughed, an awful sound rising from his lungs in some hellish catarrh. He pressed his hand flat against my chest. I refused to acknowledge as real the deathly chill seeping into my torso. It was but another trick. It had to be.

"Yes, my features are not the most discreet," he replied, a terrifying grin stretching the dead skin across his skull. "But, there is more to me than meets the eye, *Rumpelstiltskin*."

I froze. Impossible.

"How...how do you know who I am?" I finally stammered. Now that I was a man, people no longer recognized the boy they wished to forget existed.

He laughed, and the hairs on my skin rose with gooseflesh.

"I know everything about you. Your past, your future," he cooed. "Most importantly, I know the revenge growing in your heart, and how only the king's life will satisfy its hunger."

He pressed a bony finger into my chest, right where my heart pounded frantically against my ribs. There could be no denying the tug

I felt from the icy thread that now seemed to stitch itself between his finger and my flesh.

My mind reeled in panic at his statement. I had never breathed a word of my ultimate desire or of the anger boiling in my veins. How could he know? What kind of diablerie was this?

"I don't think you are quite getting it," he chuckled with a rattling of the bones in his neck. "I suppose the mortal mind can only comprehend so much. Perhaps a different form will be helpful? Yes, I think that's best."

He wrapped himself in his robe, looking like a bat waiting to be summoned back to hell. Then a hand, a perfectly formed human hand, emerged from the cloak, followed by an arm until the fabric fell to the floor, revealing a flawless body that overtook me with its magnificence.

He looked like a brave young god sculpted in the finest marble. Every muscle was beautifully formed, face radiant in glowing bronze. Demon turned angel, the only recognizable feature being his striking blue eyes.

He admired his new shape in the mirror, turning and flexing before putting on a pair of tight leather pants and covering his bare chest with a loose fitting shirt.

"I'm always astonished how humanity would rather pay for ugliness over beauty," he remarked, running his fingers through a mass of blonde hair.

My mouth fell open. I didn't know what to believe anymore.

"What are you?" I breathed.

He released a musical snicker. "I do apologize for forgetting my manners. Allow me to introduce myself. I am Fate, and you have my complete and utter attention."

His teeth shone like bright pearls, and his skin glowed in the lamplight. Once more, he ran his now-warm fingers over my chest, finding my heart and pulling that icy thread yet again. I shivered, but whether with fear or pleasure, I couldn't tell.

"You see, Rumpelstiltskin," he said. "You are quite different from your fellow man. Just moments ago they all cowered like dogs seeing me as a corpse, but not you. No, your soul is quite unique, driven by the most exquisite pain I've ever witnessed."

He gripped my chin in his strong hands almost to the point of discomfort. He examined me closely, and hunger lit up in his eyes. His grin widened as he finally released my jaw. I resisted rubbing it to try and remove the residual sensation of his fingers from my skin.

"I am only disappointed you are not using this gift to its full potential," he continued. "Pain is power, after all."

"I would hardly say pain is a gift," I replied. "Every day the king lives I am mocked, reminded I am incapable of fulfilling what I want most. After what he did..."

"I know what he did. Terribly tragic," he said, cutting me off. "I am Fate, remember? I know what happens to every living creature."

He took a seat on a pile of cushions and motioned for me to do the same. "You want vengeance?" he asked casually.

"More than anything," I replied.

"Well, you are in luck. Vengeance is a specialty of mine. The question is, how are you going to make him pay? I'm assuming with all the years you've had to think about your misery, you've been able to come up with something."

I sat dumbfounded for a moment, my mind racing with the thousands of scenarios I dreamt for the king's grisly end. There was stabbing, strangling, burning, drowning, throat slitting, and neck breaking. Each was more delicious than the next, and I couldn't choose which would be more satisfying.

"Kill him," I replied, gore swirling in my brain. "A quick twist of the neck or knife in the gut should get the job done. That's the only way I can see."

Fate tsked, his face a mask of disappointment.

"'Kill him?'" he questioned mockingly. "That is the type of answer I'd expect from a clod, but not from someone like you. Killing is far too quick an end. There's no fun, no rush of pleasure in your triumph. You need to make him suffer. Make him feel your pain. Make him understand what it means to lose what one loves most. I think that a far more satisfying plan, don't you?"

I hadn't thought of it like that. I'd only ever imagined a knife in his chest, his reign of terror finished. Quick and simple. But, suffering...

suffering opened a whole new world of opportunities I had not thought of before.

“Perhaps that does sound more rewarding,” I said with a grin. “I only see one problem.”

“Whatever would that be?”

“That man is incapable of loving anything.”

Frustration pulled on his face again.

“All men love,” he said firmly. “Men of his ilk love the strongest. They murder, battle, and destroy for love of power, wealth, and legacy. That is what causes his heart to pound and makes his soul soar. Strip him of his power, and he will suffer.”

I laughed. "That’s all fine and good, but how exactly would I ‘strip him’ of something so intangible?"

“I have a way,” he said confidently, dismissing my concerns with a wave of his hand. “I told you vengeance is my specialty. I would not seek you out if I didn’t have anything to offer. What an annoying waste of time that would be, and I hope by now you realize...I don’t waste my own time.” He leaned in, locks of blonde hair falling around his inhumanly beautiful face. “If power is to be his downfall, then power you will have. I will give you a small amount of the power I wield, and that will be enough to achieve the revenge you seek.”

His words sounded like honey. Deep within me, a hunger for the sweetness of power I hadn’t known I possessed started to grow. It pounded in my chest, thirsting for what he offered. To be honest, it terrified me.

"Why would you do that?” I asked, trying to choke down the antipathy and anticipation. “There has to be something in it for you.”

"Why must there always be a reason?” he sighed. “It’s simple. I can recognize a desperate soul, and yours is reeking. Like you, I have grown tired of Providence always ruling in the favor of kings and emperors. It’s time they understand the suffering they cause.”

"Fate chooses favorites, then?" I asked.

"Playing favorites isn’t exactly in the rules, but there are some people you just want to watch burn. The king has been allowed to cause torment far too long. I prefer to think of it as choosing judgment rather than favorites.”

Without warning he pressed his hand to my chest, his fingers stiff. He gazed impatiently at his hand, then smiled as if he saw what he had been searching for.

Pulling back, he stood up.

"You are thinking too hard about all this," he said. "This is your only opportunity, Rumpelstiltskin. I am offering you the path, granting your deepest wish. Don't you want your family avenged? I know their anguished cries still haunt your dreams. Together, we can make him pay. Make him pay for all the tragedies he has caused. Wouldn't you like your name to be cleared of the stench it's carried for so many years? To be praised a hero instead of reviled as the villain?"

Ghostly cheers of praise echoed in my head, those who hated me now loving me. Thanking me for my good deed. My name restored. My life reclaimed. And, those three hags who doubted me...now taught crystal balls are nothing but worthless glass. I craved to make his words reality.

"What are you proposing I do?" I asked.

He looked thrilled, grinning widely.

"It's quite simple really. I transfer some of my power, just a little, and you follow it to its inevitable conclusion. Give the king the wealth he desires, the power he seeks, and a legacy to grow. Then *take it all away*."

He held out his hand, waiting for me to take it. The spite in his words was exhilarating, and my skin prickled. I liked the sensation and wanted to feel it again. Without another thought, I stood and grasped his hand.

Satisfaction rippled over him, and his beauty turned devilish.

"Excellent," he commented, his grip on my hand turning from flesh to steel. "Then it is agreed. Now, just to impart to you what you need."

Forcing my hand open, he inspected my palm. He trailed his thumb in tickling circles, leaving no mound or crevice untouched. A shiver went down my spine, almost like one of pleasure. Finally, he centered his thumb, rubbing up and down the long crease that went from base to top.

"Stunning," he commented, fascinated by the line and bringing it close to his face. He pressed deeper and my heart jumped. "Your fate line shows such depth, such strength." His breath was warm against my open hand. "However, it needs to be much deeper if we want this to work."

The flash of a pair of scissors gleamed in my vision. They were exquisite with long silver blades and intricate designs that ran from handle to tip. I thought I was delirious, but I swore I heard a hum resonating from them as he opened them wide, placing the sharp blade against the crease.

"Brace yourself," he said.

The cool edge rested against the line. Then, there was nothing but hot agony. It was violent. Savage. Searing pain cut through my flesh as he etched the blade down my palm. The tip sliced skin effortlessly, scratching across bones and sinew. My vision blurred. The anguish was so intense that my vision grew dark, and the world swung back and forth.

"I know, I know. It's never very pleasant." I heard his voice pulse through my pain. "But, what's next will be the real torture."

He redoubled his grip on my hand, the torment blazing even stronger than before. Like molten iron, it spread up my arm, infecting my every muscle. But he didn't relent. He only grasped firmer. Blistering coldness came next, liquid ice surging its way into my hand and limb, following the veins until it flowed through my entire body. My lungs burned as they howled for oxygen. My heartbeats became sluggish and hopeless.

Only once the glacial mix filled me entirely did he release me.

I fell to the ground, completely drained of any warmth, unable to move even a finger. I don't know how, but I knew I was dying.

"It's normal to feel a bit peculiar. It will be gone in a moment. Your body has undergone quite the transformation! The power flowing through your veins will become legend for sure," he said with pride.

Just as I wondered when death would grant me the peace I craved, warmth slowly melted the ice. My heart beat quicker, stronger, pushing blood through my body once more. Nerves awakened, causing my skin to feel like hundreds of small worms were gliding over me. Then, all sensations stopped.

Everything changed from that point on.

The man I was had been replaced by some new force thriving within my soul.

I opened my eyes to a dazzling array of color. Smells were distinguished and unique. The entire campsite transformed into a living being, and I knew exactly where everyone was. My world was sharpened. Heightened.

Shakily, I stood, and he looked extremely pleased.

"The change is beautiful, isn't it?" he asked. Tones bled into one another.

"It's amazing," I replied, fascinated by my own voice. The world was completely new, like a dulling haze had been removed, and I saw it all for the first time.

"Now, close your eyes. Concentrate on those around you. What do you sense?"

Doing as he said I found myself outside my body, looking out over the campsite. Little flames roamed around, glowing hot. Each contained a desire or held a secret. I wanted them to be mine.

"What are they?" I asked.

"Desperate souls," he replied. "They are the most useful of all, willing to do anything just to taste what they want most."

A black quill materialized in his hand. It was smooth and glinted enticingly in the lamplight.

"You will need this," he said. "It is the only way to bind their blood to you. You will be surprised how quickly they sign their names away. Humanity will give much to gain little."

I took it eagerly, pulling the soft feather through my fingers. My newfound hunger demanded to be slaked.

"Ah, you will start collecting them soon enough," he said, seeming to notice my ravenous thoughts. "I suggest you spend time figuring out how to make the king suffer."

"You aren't going to tell me?"

He laughed.

"I can only suggest, not command. Such is the sad limit of my power. I have every confidence you will figure it out yourself." He looked pleased. "I can give you some advice, however. Moments from our past often influence our future. Perhaps think it over while spinning."

He grazed his warm fingers across my cheek. Then he vanished, and I was born a new being.

I SECLUDED myself deep in a nearby forest away from the flames I desired.

With clear mind I fashioned for myself a modest shelter. A deluge of ideas and plots soon took over. Each was more devious than the last, the smile on my lips growing as they swam through my mind. But soon, I faced a dilemma. There were too many scenarios, too many paths I could choose.

My concentration started to fade the harder I thought. Pacing back and forth, I pulled at my hair, but my mind refused to obey.

Sitting on the floor, I rubbed my eyes with my hands, hissing at the sting.

Moments from our past often influence our future

In the darkness behind my closed eyelids, I fell back into my past. I was back in that attic, spinning fluffy bits of wool for those three hags. I could feel the thread running through my fingers. Most importantly, I remembered the clarity of mind it provided.

I jumped as a spinning wheel popped into existence before me. Its wooden frame gleamed in the lamplight, perfect and complete. Was this my magic? I struggled to sense the exact firing of spells in my blood that had brought the spinning wheel to me, but there was nothing but powerful, sloshing chaos. I tried to visualize another spinning wheel popping up, but my magic refused to cooperate, producing instead a small pile of straw. Not exactly what I had hoped for.

I slid a hand over the smooth grain and sat down on the seat. Giving the wheel a spin, a comforting *whirr* filled the room. The spokes blurred together, becoming almost invisible.

"We never should have taken him in."

"You must leave us."

"It has already taken hold."

Those voices I wished to forget echoed in my mind. Their words still stung.

I gave the wheel another spin, *whirring* them away.

"Life would be much easier if we could just spin straw into gold instead!"

Those women were nothing but senseless.

And yet...

I chuckled under my breath and looked at the pile of straw next to me. Perhaps I did know what I was doing after all. I picked up a handful of the hollow twigs and began to treadle. The wheel spun faster and faster, the *whirr* surrounding me utterly. I fed the straw into its mouth, twisting the strands violently within my hands. An odd sensation took place. The straw grew thinner, smoother, harder.

To my delight, a delicate golden thread peeked through my fingers. It wrapped around the bobbin, layers of gold spinning around and around, until the spool was fat with the most beautiful thread I had ever seen.

The path to vengeance was clear and paved with gold.

THE HUNGER WAS INSATIABLE NOW. I couldn't sleep, couldn't even congratulate myself on creating the perfect plan. I could only think of the flames.

Though it had taken some time to master my magic, I now commanded it with a savage ease. The only hitch was that the stronger the magic I used, the more I needed the fuel of others' despair.

My first few attempts at making a contract were clumsy, and more than once, I went away hungry and unfulfilled. I was a quick study, though. One doesn't survive long as an outcast without wits, and whereas I had had sharp wits before, I now had a knife's edge cunning. Soon enough, I was practiced in getting what I wanted by giving fools what they wanted.

It was time to return to the castle town, to begin to card the wool of deceit in preparation for spinning the thread of King Edward's noose.

I went to where I knew I could surely find the willing: the most disreputable tavern I could find. Walking through the doors, desperate souls surrounded me. A cacophony of voices and heartbeats wanted, needed... craved. My body vibrated, pushing me to feed upon them.

One burned brighter than the rest. My prey hid inside.

The tavern was like another world. The stench of old sweat, old beer, and old smoke hung in the air, and rolls of dice clattered across tables as voices rose in competing tall tales. Then I saw him, the flame I hungered for burning prettily in his soul.

He was a young man dressed in the plain armor of a guard. Blonde hair was shorn close to his scalp, and his frame was rock solid. But what took my notice was the map of scars etched across his face. His hopelessness was electrifying. The pounding in my head was unbearable now. I had to have him.

Taking a deep breath, I sat down next to him at the bar, shoving away a collection of empty pints. He seemed surprised, though his eyes wandered ever so slightly from drink.

"Why so glum?" I asked.

"Piss off," he grunted, downing the rest of his mug.

I ordered him another, which seemed to afford me a few more moments of his attention.

"Come, come," I said, feigning concern. "Tell me. Sometimes sharing with a stranger is better than all your loved ones listening."

He sighed. Sadness bubbled within his heart.

"There is no hope," he replied. "I'll never win Evelyn's hand."

He took the beer I ordered him and quickly drank it empty.

"So, it is the woman?" I asked. It always was.

"No. It is her father."

"Ah, and you think ale is going to make him approve of you more?"

He shot me a dirty look, slamming the mug down. Frankly, as far as tantrums rated, this was pathetic and nowhere near enough to put me off my prey.

"I can help you," I offered casually.

The youth barked out a bitter laugh. "There's not a thing you can do."

"That may be true for you and for everyone else in this miserable little tavern-" the barmaid shot me a dirty look, "-but I am different than everyone else." I said.

He rubbed his eyes. "You can say that again," I heard him say under his breath.

"Helping others helps me. I thrive on...solving problems. Believe me, I can help you," I encouraged.

He only scoffed and crossed his arms. "Help me? How could you help someone with no chance in life? I am nothing. Never will be. And, the woman I love will marry the bailiff's son because her papa told her to."

I tried to pay attention to his jabber, but his despair was such an absolute blaze now I found it increasingly difficult. I tasted it. Craved it.

"You'd be surprised what I am capable of," I said, lowering my voice. "Just name it, and I can make it happen."

He laughed now, slipping sloppily around on the barstool. His mood, no doubt due to the prodigious consumption of ale, slipped just as sloppily from frustration to amusement

"You'd make a damn fine mummer," he chortled. "I nearly believed you."

"Well, it is a shame you don't believe, because you are missing out on the opportunity of your life. You're letting Evelyn go without even a fight. Maybe her father is right. You don't deserve her. You are nothing but a coward." It was ridiculously easy to use his very words to goad him to my purpose.

Two strong hands wrapped around my collar and jerked me off my stool. His breath stank.

"I do deserve her, you hear!" he shouted, flecks of his spit hitting my face.

"Then prove it. Hear me out. That's all I ask," I said calmly.

His rage lessened and he unrolled his fists, releasing my collar. We both sank back onto the stools.

"What if I were to make you captain of the guard?" I whispered. "You would get a nice living. You might even achieve being respectable. Would that impress her father?"

He laughed again. Red flushed his face, making his web of white scars stand out even more.

"I suppose it would," he said. He leaned in and murmured, "Are you...are you from the castle? Do you know someone who can do this?"

I chuckled at his simple brain. No imagination, that was for sure.

"I am more powerful than anyone at the castle," I told him. "And, today is your lucky day."

I moved him back with my arm and cleared a space on the bar. His eyes nearly popped out of his head as he watched a piece of parchment appear in my hand. Letting it unroll, the terms of our deal were laid out neat and tight. He looked up at me as if I were a ghost, wearing an odd expression of horror mixed with fascination.

"What are you?" he asked, slapping a hand against his forehead.

"That doesn't matter," I answered airily. "What does matter is what I told you. Now, pay attention. This contract specifies that you will become captain of the guard, have a life actually worth living, and can marry that woman you seem so smitten with. All you have to do is sign."

I pulled out the black quill Fate gave me, my heart beating into my throat, eager for his blood.

"Let me get this straight," he said slowly. "All I have to do is sign my name, and you will give me all this?"

"Exactly," I said, impatience electrifying my body.

He took the quill. "I'm no fool," he stated. "You can't just be granting wishes for free. What do you want in return? I don't have much money."

"Smart man! Always best to ask questions before you sign," I replied, hiding my annoyance that he finally found the working part of his brain. "Money is of no use to me. Silence, however, that is hard to come by these days. For my price, all I ask is you don't tell a soul about this night or me. Understood?" I lowered my voice. "If you break our contract, I swear to you worse awaits you than anything you could ever imagine."

He nodded his head and stared for a moment at the quill. I sat back and waited, moistening my lips for the moment I sought. Finally, he lowered the quill to the page. The instant tip touched paper, euphoria rushed over my body. I fed on his despair with every letter he scribbled. My fingers and toes tingled with pleasure, my core coiled in warmth. I was floating, filled with beautiful intoxication until I was utterly replete. Whole.

I loved it.

Only once he dropped the quill did the flame within him finally extinguish. His despair was now mine, and my hunger was slaked.

He gave a hiss, looking at his fingertips. "What the devil was that?" he asked, his breaths hard from shock.

"A bit harsh, I know, but blood is the only way to ensure you uphold your end of the bargain." I chuckled.

"Blood?" he asked.

"What else did you expect? Butterflies?"

I looked at his name gleaming in crimson. A smile pulled on my lips, enjoying the residual exhilaration from the experience.

"Now Rowan," I said, putting the contract and quill in my pocket. "Why are you wasting time worrying over nothing more than a pin-prick, when you could be enjoying your new uniform?"

He looked down and his mouth fell open. His entire uniform had changed. No longer did he wear the dark gray and chainmail of a simple guard. Now he was clothed in bright reds and shiny plates of armor. A golden lion roared on the front of his breastplate.

"I really am a captain now!" he exclaimed. He stood, still swaying a bit from the alcohol flooding his veins. I doubted he would be so friendly had he been sober. He shook my hand furiously.

"I am going to go to Evelyn's father and ask for her hand. Let's see him tell me I'm not worth the dung beneath his boot now."

He left with an expression of great joy, and I sank back into the shadows. I looked out at the other flames surrounding me and I realized there was no reason I couldn't find my unsuspecting pawns here. The place reeked of desperation, everyone clawing to get out of the muck they were destined to wallow in.

All I required was a fool, and my plan could be set in motion.

CHAPTER SIX

WEDDING BELLS: LAILA

Without so much as a goodbye, he disappeared back into the nothingness from which he came. I assured myself I could not have been happier to be rid of him. He was arrogant. Insufferable. But, the lingering sensation of his lips on mine remained, and it irritated me as much as it burned me.

"My lady, if you would hold your breath for a moment more, we will finish lacing you in," Rosamund, my new lady-in-waiting, instructed.

I did as she said and tried to look pleasant as I saw my reflection in the mirror. Today was my wedding day, and I would be made queen. That strange man, whoever he was, might have saved my neck from the noose, but I would direct and shape my own life now. I was absolutely determined not to waste another thought on him.

"Look at her! What a perfect portrait of happiness."

If only the maids and ladies knew what caused the happiness filling my veins. Layers of colorful silks and velvets kissed my skin. Rouge brightened my cheeks and lips. Exotic perfume rose from between my breasts.

"You look beautiful, my lady!" Rosamund exclaimed, placing a crown of orange blossoms atop my hair. Soon enough, it would be replaced with gold and rubies.

I took one last look at my reflection. I ran my fingers down the smooth fabric, and the thrill of it chilled my bones. The king was at my mercy now, the mercy of the miller's daughter.

Like a shadow in the midday sun, unease stirred at the back of my mind. There was a quick, blaring pang of panic—what was I doing in marrying this evil man?—followed by another fluttering of doubt. I had signed away my firstborn literally to a stranger. Was that right? Was that fair? Could I trust him?

The bells began to ring, and I shoved my fears back, hefting them as if they were so many sacks of flour. The choices were made. There was no time to question and even less time to answer. I clung to the belief that I was a good person. As if to expiate my future sins, I vowed in that moment to become a good and noble queen who served and protected her people.

"My lady?" Rosamund asked tentatively.

I nodded and allowed her and the other ladies to lift up my train and escort me to the chapel in the palace. All along the halls, courtiers and even servants lined up to make their obeisance to me. I bestowed small smiles and quick nods as I passed them, feeling myself more and more a queen with each step.

The royal chapel was full to capacity with guests jostling for position without regard for their colorful velvets, silks, and furs. The air was thick with incense and the smell of a thousand beeswax candles burning brightly. Dizzy and nervous, I matched my steps to the cadence of the liturgical music that filled the space, bouncing off the walls and vaulted ceilings.

After what felt like an age, I reached the altar. The king held his hand out for me, and I took it, allowing him to lead me the final steps to the kneeling bench. I saw the king in his cloak of red velvet and golden thread. I saw his smile beneath his dark beard. I saw his green eyes alight with satisfaction.

But, truly, all I could see was all the gold. It was everywhere. Every surface of the chapel was gilded, as was the bishop himself, his robes so stiff with gold thread that he could hardly move in them. I thought of the stranger's hands twisting straw into golden thread.

The ceremony began, and a tumble of ancient words fell from the priest's mouth. We performed the prayers and recitations as devoutly as any monk or nun. However, I dared not look into the face of our Lord on the crucifix. Our marriage was a mockery. There was no love, no devotion. Only pain and power were worshipped at our altar. A ring slid over my finger. A crown of gold and rubies crushed the orange blossoms in my hair. Cheers erupted all around, hailing me as their queen. For better or worse, it was done.

THE FEAST that followed could have fed a village for an entire year. As insistent as the hum of discomfort was in my soul, I couldn't help but be swept away by the magnificence of the spectacle. For, indeed, it was a spectacle, with the entrance of the food heralded by trumpets, drums, and applause.

I was astounded by the extravagance, watching the seemingly endless parade of dishes. First came the rich, herb-encrusted roasts of boar, venison, and fowl. Then followed pies so large that they needed two servants to carry them. Sheer enormity soon gave way to the fantastic as mythical beasts on golden platters made their entrance. Heads and torsos of peacocks were sewn onto the haunches of pigs, the feathers and plumes remaining intact. It was monstrous yet beautiful.

"How is one to eat that?" I whispered.

"These were creatures created in the kitchens only for the amusement of the guests," the king, or rather, my husband Edward replied. "That's the fabled Pavosus. Can't have a proper feast without one or two of those."

The servants presented it before us, and I marveled such barbaric artistry, though my practical peasant side deplored the senseless waste of such animals. I didn't have long to mull over my morals, as the feast began in earnest, and I was forced to sample every dish. At least, I would not go hungry again. I found myself unexpectedly thankful for such small mercies.

Another parade began after the main courses were finished. Tottering towers of confectionary and cake perfumed the air with vanilla and cinnamon. I even saw chocolate for the first time, and I was eager to sample it. After the pastry came servants bearing golden bowls of exotic fruits, and I exclaimed in pleasure when a page placed a dish of figs on the table.

I had never tasted a fig before and my mouth began to water, curious of the fruit's fabled sweetness. I reached out to pluck one from the dish, but Edward brushed my hand aside. Instead, he picked up the fruit and held it to my lips.

"Your first time?" he asked, and I knew he was asking about more than my culinary experience.

"Yes," I said, suddenly irritated and nervous. "The life I lived before did not allow for such frivolities. The more extravagant the pleasure, the higher the price there was to pay. For such as me, there was only work and death, and death was often a blessing you prayed for."

He chuckled and took a delicate bite of the fig before returning it to my lips. "You are so droll. Only work and death. One might say that about any station in life, especially one that holds the responsibility for an entire kingdom. Yet, we are born craving pleasure as well. Why else would we work?"

"To sustain ourselves," I replied. "To provide food and shelter."

"But are not food and shelter pleasures in their simplest forms?"

I stared at him, uncertain as to how to answer.

"Taste the fig, Laila," Edward commanded gently.

I did as he asked and was rewarded by a burst of crisp sweetness with an undercurrent of honey.

"You must learn how to take pleasure in your life," Edward said, setting down the fig and caressing my cheek. "And I shall have the pleasure of being your most devoted teacher."

I shivered with new and nameless sensations at his touch. It was not like the rush of exhilaration I had experienced with the stranger. No! I would not think of him. I abhorred him. I abhorred Edward. I abhorred myself. Blood bound me to one man, and a ring bound me to another.

Edward's smile deepened at my reaction, and I reminded myself that done is done. My only choice now was to embrace the choices I had made. Grabbing a fresh fig from the dish, I sunk my teeth into the supple flesh. A seductive combination of velvet sweetness filled my mouth. I wondered if what awaited me later tonight with Edward would be equally as satisfying.

"Ah!" he exclaimed, turning from me to watch the entrance of the entertainers. "Now, this shall be a real treat for you, my love."

An old man carrying a lute came to stand in the center of the room and bowed deeply to us. It took me a moment to realize he was bowing to me because I was a queen now. He looked so impossibly frail and bent that I worried the weight of the lute would cause him to topple over. It was difficult to detect which of the thousand wrinkles on his face were his eyes and lips.

"Who is he?" I asked as the man tuned his instrument.

"The most celebrated minstrel in all the kingdoms. Voice like an angel, and tales that will cause you to tremble."

I was about to ask further, but Edward placed a silencing finger on my lips. I resisted the urge to bite it off. The minstrel closed his eyes and a hush fell over the room. Then, he sent a commanding hand sweeping down the strings, creating such a mournful sound my very soul shook.

> A maiden once lived in dire scarcity,
> Wishing to be free from such misery.
> A scheming witch hearing her plea,
> Offered to rescue her for a fee.

His words tore through me as his hands continued moving swiftly up and down the shaft of the lute. Strings bent and cried out in unison with his seductive voice.

> "Give me your child," the witch demanded,
> "And I will I save you from your soot and ashes."
> Under cover of night she took such a deal,
> To trade her firstborn for a life she'd hold dear.

I tried to focus on the melody and not the words, but his voice burned each note and letter onto my heart. The tips of my fingers where the stranger's magical quill had drawn my blood began to tingle.

> The witch threw back her head and cackled with
> delight,
> Happily changing the young maiden's plight.
> Yet, once fair maiden had all that she wished,
> She refused the steep price with a wave of her wrist.

My fingers stung now as if I had plunged a hundred needles into them. The verses cracked my composure, and I bit my lip to stifle a groan.

> The price is too high, she claimed undaunted,
> Her dear child no longer unwanted.

I swore that the fire was burning the flesh of my fingers away. If I were to dare to look down, surely all I would see were char and bone. My heart pounded and my breaths grew shallow and suffocating.

> The witch unpleased by an act so brazen,
> Took vengeance on the ungrateful maiden,
> And cast her back out to her soot and ashes.
> A fate surely worse than a thousand lashes.

I saw the stranger within the song, there was no denying it anymore. All it would take was one mistake before all I had gained would turn to dirt...or straw.

Thankfully, the song ended with that. Trying not to cringe outwardly, I looked down and saw my hand, perfect and whole. The burning had vanished. My skin was cool and soft. My heart slowed, returning to steady and fluid thumps.

The old man took several seesawing bows to the thunderous applause of the court. My world once again became calm, though the warning in the song had taken up residence with my doubts in the recesses of my mind.

It was only a song. A coincidence. Resolve pounded through my veins that I would not make the same mistake as that impuissant maiden. My deal with the stranger would stand. Giving up everything I earned because of a change of heart would not be how my tale ended. Popping another fig in my mouth, I reminded myself that I was no poor maiden. I was a queen, and had I not promised to wield my power for the good of my people?

"That song pleases you, I see," Edward remarked, his gaze fixed on my mouth.

"Very much," I replied. "It reminds me of what I don't want to be. Weak."

His eyes darkened again, that hunger common to all men shining through. Weakness would be to delay any further the fulfillment of at least one of the promises I had made. If I truly didn't want to be the maiden, to be weak, I had to own it fully.

Steeling myself, I placed my hand on top of his and said, "I think it time we depart, you promised me new sensations, and I don't want to miss a moment."

His fingers wrapped around my hand, and we stood from the table. Cheers erupted as we departed.

"All hail the king and queen!"

He led me back to his apartments, which were across the hall from the queen's chambers where but this morning I had stood relishing a reprieve from the noose. After tonight, those chambers would belong entirely to me.

Edward's rooms were exactly as I imagined, as dark as his soul, and as masculine as the mask he wore. Not surprisingly, everything was done in heavy wood and the motif of crimson and gold ruled. A massive, curtained, four-poster bed stood near a roaring fire. My husband nodded curtly to the two pages who stood silently in the doorway, dismissing them. With a final bow, they closed the doors behind us. Despite my resolve for courage, my heart skipped a beat.

Edward prodded the fire several times with the poker, large plumes of sparks rolling up into the chimney. His features grew more handsome in the play between light and darkness.

"I won't deny how loathsome a creature I first found you," he said, plunging the poker deeper into the crumbling wood. "Weaseling your way into making yourself my queen. Holding my gold for ransom."

As if I felt any different about him, but I pushed my animosity away. Now was not the time. I didn't particularly rejoice at the idea of intimacy with Edward, but I wouldn't be ruled by my hatred of him. I would hold firm to what I had won. Tonight, he would take my innocence, but I would conquer a king. I admit that there was a certain viciousness about the idea that electrified me.

Standing up and moving from the hearth, he approached me and cupped my face in his hands. The green of his eyes glittered in the firelight. The heat from his fingers fed the flush in my cheeks. I closed my eyes, savoring my coming triumph.

Slowly, he slid his hands down my neck and shoulders until they circled my waist and drew me to him. His breaths were hot on my skin and stirred something restless inside me, something...unfinished. Through my eyelashes, I saw the shadows playing over his face. Yet, perhaps the shadows were tricking me, for it was another face I saw in the darkness now.

The stranger.

The ghost of his memory made me shiver with twisted desire. The stranger's features grew vibrant and clear when I closed my eyes. I could see his pale skin flushed with lust. The storms raging behind his eyes wanted me and nothing else. He refused to leave my thoughts, even though qualms of disloyalty flittered weakly around him.

Edward's lips grazed mine as he continued to speak unhurriedly. "I wanted to crush that skull of yours. Keep your insolent mind from ever forming another insolent thought again."

I only felt the stranger's lips skate down my neck leaving behind a trail of fire. Edward's words melted away as I fell further into my fantasy. Yearning built heat within my core, growing hotter with every touch. Edward's large hands no longer roved over me, only the slender fingers of the man who liberated me. He moved down my body and unlaced my gown, exposing my thirsting skin. I gasped as he gently caressed my naked breasts just as the thread that spun through his hands.

"But," he whispered, and I no longer knew if it was the stranger's voice or Edward's I heard. "I see how wrong I was for ever having thought such a thing. We are the same, you and I. We both will go to any length to get what we want."

I thrashed against a million hands as the stranger sucked my nipple into his mouth.

"You are perfect, Laila," one of them said.

Flesh blazed between my thighs and I rocked myself against the firm body pressing into me. As he lowered me to the soft bed, my lips were finally taken in a deep kiss. The stranger rolled his tongue in my mouth, and I grabbed his hair, pulling him tighter to me. Gasps echoed through the black as his hardness pushed into me, causing a warm sensation to ripple through my body. Waves of pleasure crashed over me as I moaned into the sheets.

"Pain is power," the stranger's voice rang through my head, and I realized he wasn't really there.

Yes, I reminded myself as I opened my eyes and saw Edward making me his.

Pain is power.

CHAPTER SEVEN

Whorl:

noun: The weighted part of a dropspindle that helps it to spin.
Also the spindle pulley that regulates the speed of a spinning wheel spindle

noun: A circular arrangement of like parts around an axis.

EVER AFTER: LAILA

The stranger always appeared whenever the king took me. I heard his voice. Felt his touch. Melted into his kiss. I didn't know what it meant, or if it meant anything at all. My memories of him were confusing and consuming, but, I refused to examine the matter further. After all, other than this one irritating detail, life truly became all I had wished.

I no longer had to rise with the rooster, plagued in the morning by night's icy chill. There were no more clouds of dust and dirt from the mill filling my eyes and lungs. Even my hands that were long obscured by calluses from years of grinding stones and gunnysacks softened. Now I bathed in milk and rose petals. I took long walks in the garden, enjoying the reverent bows of my subjects. I ate meat whenever I wished and drank the finest wines.

Ever mindful of my vows to myself, I endeavored to learn the royal history of my kingdom, struggling daily and dutifully with etiquette and a thousand unimportant dates when rich people had done a thousand unimportant things. More than book learning, though, I made it a point to visit orphanages and churches, encouraging charity in my subjects by bringing charity myself.

I must have seen a hundred girls like me, waiting outside the churches and peeking out from workroom windows. Their dry hair, splotchy skin, and leaden gazes were far too familiar to me. The stranger's sly laugh echoed in my mind.

I didn't need memories of him to remind me just how precarious my position was. Though they would not dare to do so openly, I could feel the scorn from the other courtiers—born noble to this life and inured to its gifts and challenges. If their bows and curtsies dipped a fraction lower to each other than to me, it was never so in the sight of the king. It did not take a clever man like the stranger to tell me that there were no doubt many plots afoot to oust me from the peacock's throne and return me to sparrowdom.

The other reminder of my fragile state of fortune was my husband himself. Edward spoiled my joy, though he gave me little reason to feel so. He looked at me with a mix of adoration and lust. You may think it sad that I found the lust easiest to accept and live with, perhaps because I felt it was his only true expression of emotion. The adoration came from his belief that we shared greed as the bedrock of our characters. He adored me as one snake adores another. Yet, I refused to define my nature by greed. Maybe it was sophistry, but I would only admit to an ironclad will to survive.

The king was assiduous in his duties as a new husband, and the results were to be expected.

"Ouch!" I exclaimed as Rosamund tightened my corset.

"Your majesty?" she queried, for I had never complained from the trussing.

"Leave my stays loose at the top," I ordered. "My breasts are tender this morning."

"Yes, your majesty."

Two days later, I refused all eggs, declaring them to be the most revolting of foods, and instead demanding nothing but smoked fish for luncheon...and supper...and breakfast.

A week later, even smoked fish palled, and I became accustomed to becoming ill at the thought of anything but weak tea. I was too tired to pay my visits, declaring the orphans and priests would have to get along without me, for I could not and would not rise from this bed.

At these words, doctors were sent for, though I hardly needed them. Perhaps refined noblewomen would have been mystified by my symptoms, but a peasant is not so easily fooled having lived a life in far closer proximity to birth and death.

I was to be a mother.

"My heir!" Edward cooed, reverently rubbing my belly. "The throne secured at last. The line of my father and his fathers will remain unbroken. You deserve every veneration, my dear."

He kissed my cheek and did not notice the bitterness behind my smile. His moment of pride and peace would be short lived. His little heir would not remain his for very long, and this thought was all that stoked the feebly floundering ember of my rage.

Perhaps my own pride and peace was quietly effacing the hard motives and harder feelings that had driven my decisions before this babe took up residence in my belly. Little movements demanded my attention, but I resolutely ignored each one, even as I repeated my mantra that I was doing this child a service. In giving it up, I was rescuing it from a corrupt father and a sham of a mother.

I rehearsed the moment I would tell the king his heir was gone. I reached for and clutched at the thought of his misery to reinforce my wavering will. He would be livid, threaten me and damn me to hell, but in the end he would not touch me. He wouldn't risk losing his gold over a child, especially not when he believed I could turn it all back into straw with a snap of my fingers. He never need know the rest of the truth about what really took place down in the dungeon. Besides, he could always use my body to produce another heir...and another. I felt sick at the thought.

As I was eating my breakfast one morning, looking out of the window at the rolling hills of the countryside, I felt one solid, determined little kick. It might as well have been a knife to my heart. I was undone. In that small, insistent announcement of my babe's sentience and existence, my power dwindled back into fear, and I was that insufferably scared peasant girl again, trapped within stone in a cage of straw.

My dreams were no longer soft and easy. Now, there were only nightmares filled with those storms of the stranger's gray eyes. Every night, I saw his fingers turn to claws, reaching out for my child. Flashes of gold like lightning thundered above me as I begged for forgiveness, but in these dreams, none was given.

❧

"HERE'S the cloak you requested, your majesty," Rosamund said.

She placed the heavy fabric around my shoulders with deference, but her expression was disapproving. I stared unblinkingly at my reflection as I rubbed a hand over my swollen belly.

"Are you sure you want to be walking about the gardens, your majesty?" she asked, fastening the gold clasp around my throat. "You seem rather pale. It might be better for you to remain indoors. We could bring a settee to the window if you desired fresh air. Your ladies worry that you walk entirely too much for a woman as heavy with child as you are."

Being with child had not improved my temper, and it was only my constant vigilance that kept me from lashing out and being snappish.

"I know you are only trying to be helpful," I said after a deep, calming breath. "I shall be confined indoors soon enough when the babe and the snows come. Winter comes quickly." These last words came quietly, and I did not speak of the weather.

Understanding flooded Rosemund's expression and she gave a quick nod, opening the door.

"Do you want me to accompany you?" she asked timidly.

"No thank you," I answered. "I wish to be alone."

I enjoyed the freedom of the garden away from the stifling castle. I'd been suffering from slight pains all day. The child would soon come, and with it, a battle I knew every woman faced but not every woman won. The sun was warm against my skin, the light burning away the claws that chased me in my nightmares. I took quick steps, eager for the refuge the flowers and shrubs granted, and I hoped if I ventured deep enough, I would never be found.

I wandered away from the other courtiers. Leaves rustled and their shadows danced among the golden pebbles underfoot. Roses swayed in the breeze. I sat on an iron bench and closed my eyes. But as with all good things, there is always an end. A rush of fabric rustled beside me.

"What is troubling you?" Edward questioned, sitting next to me. "Of late, you seem to want nothing else but to walk the grounds for hours on end. I'm beginning to think you're a ghost."

He grimaced and touched his hand to my forehead, checking for a sign of fever. Checking if he should be concerned his gold would return to straw.

"The babe's movements make it difficult to stay still with any comfort," I replied, waving his hand away.

"I would think you would be more at ease upon your bed."

"I shall tie a sack with a small, kicking spaniel to your stomach, and then we shall see how much ease you find," I said, fighting to contain the surge of snappishness that rose up in me.

"I think you are afraid," Edward said simply.

I stared at him, unable to think of quick words of denial.

"You were so joyful when you discovered you were with child. But now, I watch fear crippling you like a disease. I've spent many a night wondering the reason, and it occurred to me. I know."

I forced my expression to remain stoic. "What do you mean?" I asked.

"What I mean to say is what torments you is simply what torments all women. You fear the pains of childbirth."

"I am not afraid of pain," I said.

"Then, you must be afraid of motherhood itself. I have heard it is common for new mothers to worry about their ability to care for a child. You are afraid you will not be adequate."

A single tear rolled down my cheek, and I cursed myself for allowing such weakness to overcome me again. I already abhorred the mother I was, abandoning my unborn child for a taste of wealth and power.

"No, that's not it," I said, unable to stop the flow of my words. "It's not fear for myself. It's fear for the child."

"The child? But whatever for?" he chuckled.

I couldn't tell him the truth, but I could speak close enough to it. "You tell me that as king, you do not fear that danger waits around every corner, ready to snatch away all you love in an instant?"

His chuckle turned into a laugh. I shifted uncomfortably on the bench. My back had begun to ache.

"Is that all?" he asked. "You give me too little credit for being able to protect what is mine. I assure you nothing will happen to our child as long as I am king."

He caressed my stomach, pausing to feel the babe kicking. I thought I had finally lost control of my temper and had pissed myself in rage, for there was a snapping cramp inside me, and something wet ran down my legs.

Another low, prolonged ache followed, leaving me weak and breathless. I knew then that the time had come. Apparently, Edward had guessed as much as well.

"Let's get you back," he said, sweeping me up into his arms, and for once, I was grateful for my husband's strength and vigor. "I think we might meet our new heir before the day is through!"

Edward held me fast through another two contractions as he carried me up to my rooms. He laid me on the bed and kissed my brow before midwives banned him from the room. With practiced efficiency, they had changed me into a nightgown and braided my hair. They pressed and prodded my shuddering belly to determine the babe's position, and they peered between my legs to see how ready I was.

Hours passed and candles were lit. The pain came and went in ever-quicker rounds, until the near-constant agony caused my vision to go black. The child was fighting for its release into the world.

I could no longer hear my own screams. All I knew was darkness and pain beyond anything imaginable. When I could finally, push, I swore the pressure would crush my body, grinding my bones to grit and grain.

And then, it was over. There was a final spasm of agony, a strange whooshing sensation, and instant relief. In a daze, I heard my child's cry.

"It's a boy! A prince!" Rosamund yelped excitedly in my ear.

The room gained clarity with each passing moment. A squirming little red, wrinkly thing was handed to me. Looking down, I saw nothing but perfection. For the first time in my life, I fell in love. In that moment, I knew I could not give up this child. I stared at a little nose and little fingers. It was a life. A complete life I was destined to care for.

> The price is too high, she claimed undaunted,
> Her dear child no longer unwanted.
> The witch unpleased by an act so brazen,
> Took vengeance on the ungrateful maiden,
> And returned her back to her soot and ashes.
> A fate surely worse than a thousand lashes.

The song tumbled through my head as I kissed his forehead and cheeks. That maiden might have returned to soot and ash, but I was not that maiden. No longer would I be ruled by fear. Love—the best, truest kind of love—would now give me the power I needed. The child would never be alone, never unprotected. I had already faced the stranger once and got him to bend to my wishes. There was no reason I couldn't do it again. I would fight for my child, and I would win.

"Do not worry, Tristan. You have a mother's love and a mother's protection," I cooed, kissing his nose. "I won't let anything happen to you. I promise."

CHAPTER EIGHT

Noun. The device on a spinning wheel for adding a twist to yarn.

Noun (informal). A long jump or leap.

EVER AFTER: RUMPELSTILTSKIN

Bells rang out from every church tower in a cacophony of cheer, announcing the birth of the king's heir.

"A prince! A prince! Long live the King and Queen! A prince!"

So many drunken fools attempted to sing and dance while holding cups, streams of ale and wine flowed through the streets like blood through arteries. They proclaimed themselves the most loving and devoted subjects of the king and queen, and boasted with ignorant pride of the size and health of the little baby prince that even now was no doubt shitting his nappies.

I curled my lips in disgust as I watched them. How blind they all were, celebrating the very nobility that kept them firmly beneath their boots, ground into poverty, illness, and illiteracy. The insignificant wretches would soon finally see how blind they were to the evils of the monarch they now celebrated.

I had waited nearly a year for the little wailing worm to grow inside Laila, waiting until its little lungs screamed and wailed, making the king a proud father. Ah, the king! How he would hold that little bundle of noise tightly and imagine summer evenings spent playing with wooden swords. Imagine an army of pretty horses trotting through forests as his son grew into a skilled huntsman. Imagine forming great alliances with other countries who wanted to marry off their beautiful princesses to the handsome prince.

I could see it now. So many memories to be made. So many memories I would never allow. The king's legacy at last was mine to take, just as he had taken my own. Oh, without a doubt, he would take Laila back to his bed in desperation to produce another heir, but everyone would always know that child would be a second-born, the Damoclean sword of the missing true heir always hanging over their heads.

There was always the chance that the king would discover Laila's complicity in the plot to steal his heir and kill her. That was the one risk I couldn't quite figure out how to manage. It wasn't that I wanted to save her from any goodness of my heart. No, she was worth saving because she was clever, and I always had a use for clever people. Besides, she was actually turning out to be a decent queen, and the people deserved at least one monarch who wasn't a monster.

"Did ye hear the news?" a drunken man exclaimed, attempting to embrace me and sending beer sloshing over the rim of his mug and onto my tunic. "There's to be a masked ball fer the prince! Can you imagine such an evening? The food, the drink?"

"I'd say you've had more on your own than the nobles could hope to consume together," I replied, cleaning the mess on my shirt with a subtle wave of my fingers.

The drunk stared out as if seeing a hundred dancers right in front of us, his mouth hanging open dreamily.

"What I wouldn'e give ter be there tonight among all those pretty ladies and proper gentlemen. Just a chance ter see the new heir would be a dream come true," he wished. Tears streamed down the dirt encrusting his cheeks, and he blew his nose on a handkerchief greyed by a thousand washes. "But, I can't blame them fer not wanting us simple folk. Wouldn'e know the first thing how ter dance with such company, probably give all those nobles a right shock tromping on their fine shoes. Naw, they were right not wanting us. Embarrass his majesty, it would! We can't have that on such a special day. Wouldn'e be right."

Though he was an idiot, he presented a rather interesting scenario too tempting to ignore. Such a public demonstration was just the thing that would make crushing the king all the more delectable. How awfully embarrassing for his majesty indeed!

THE LONG DEAD PAST: HOW IT ALL BEGAN

"You're running too fast!" my sister called complainingly after me, her short legs struggling to catch up with me on my longer ones. Even as a child, I had run to length.

"That's the point in a race, Madelin," I replied.

Fresh air surged into my lungs with every breath until two hands grabbed hold of my arm. The hard ground came up fast to meet me as I fell to the ground, a small body slamming onto me.

"Got you!" she squealed.

"Only because you made me fall," I replied, tweaking her nose.

"What else do you expect me to do? You are five years older and five years taller. I don't have any chance of winning unless I try to be a bit more creative."

"And, by creative, you mean cheating?" I snorted.

"All that matters is that I won."

Ringlets of blonde hair framed a victorious expression that was too sweet to be anywhere near smug. She had worn the same expression as a babe when she was first placed in my arms, as if she was inordinately proud of the triumph of her birth. Her exultance was always infectious, and I had fallen under her spell in that first moment. I was her devotee, worshipping my burbling little goddess and sworn to her protection with all my boyish fervor.

Hooking her bodily under one arm, I stood, hauling her with me like a very small sack of potatoes. To her impotent fury, I even nonchalantly stooped to brush the grass off my knees while still holding her thus. Her ire didn't fool me, and soon enough, her giggles broke through like the brilliant sun through half-hearted clouds.

She squirmed against my grip, and I relented, gently setting her on her dirty little bare feet. Mother despaired of getting Madelin to wear even the softest kid slippers. Madelin would simply argue that she could not feel the earth through her shoes, and bless my mother, she understood what her little girl was trying to say.

Madelin looked out over the valley, shielding her eyes from the sun's glare.

"I always love seeing all the farmhouses from up here," she said. "They look so small. Sometimes, I like to pretend that families of ants live there."

"If they are ants to us, what do we look like to them?"

"Very big ants." It was impossible not to laugh at her solemn logic.

Still, there was some undeniable rationale behind her words, given the sheer size of Barschloss Court, the Rumpelstiltskin family home for centuries. Rows of expensively leaded windows gleamed in the afternoon light. Great stone walls stood tall and stern against a vibrant green lawn. The angled roof was crowned by a collection of haphazard chimneys that scraped the sky.

"I can't imagine this will all be mine one day," I said with a happy sigh. "I'll be a great Lord, and go hunting every day without worrying about bedtime."

"And I'll marry a prince, but only if he is handsome," Madelin chimed in.

I couldn't help but laugh and ruffled her hair. A warm summer breeze caused her skirts to billow behind her and she very nearly looked like one of those princesses she so wanted to be.

"I don't think you need to worry about engagements for a while. You are only seven, after all. For now, I think it best we get back. Father should be home any minute."

I offered her my hand and she happily took it as we crossed the grounds back to the castle. I had lost count how many days we spent playing in these lawns and gardens for the joyous hours had seemed endless as we galloped around on sticks as our noble steeds, surveying our lands, and offering benevolence to our invisible subjects.

"Father always seems to be gone with the king," Madelin said with a small frown.

"That's because he is important," I replied with an air of adult superiority. "King Edward is having trouble at court. He's already executed several good-for-nothings. He needs father's help to make sure his throne remains safe."

"How do you know all that?" she asked.

I paused.

"I...overheard father and mother talking about it," I finally admitted.

Her face twisted into one of hearty disapproval.

"Henry, you know eavesdropping is bad."

"It is the only way to learn anything interesting," I retorted. "Father says the courtiers do it all the time. When you are bigger, you'll learn that important men such as father and myself must sometimes do these things in order to protect what is ours.

She sighed and shook her head. "I wouldn't do it. You might hear something you don't much like."

"What might you not like?" Mother's voice asked as we tumbled through the front entrance.

"Nothing," I blurted out in an incredibly unconvincing manner.

She narrowed her gray eyes, and her pretty face grew sharp. However, given that both of us were in one piece, our clothes were not (too) dirty, and no one had complained of broken china, shoeless horses returning to the stables, or any other mayhem that day, she must have figured that our secrets were not yet that terrible. She wrapped us in a large hug, kissing us on both of our cheeks.

Our tender moment was interrupted by a commotion in the courtyard, and we all hurried back out. There could be only one arrival that would cause such a fuss this day.

Father sat astride his chestnut palfrey, his boots and sturdy travel cloak stained with mud and dust. Yet, all the dirt from all the roads couldn't have hidden the merry expression in his blue eyes or the warrior's set of his broad shoulders.

"You have come back sooner than expected!" Mother cried, and I wondered why her voice sounded fearful even though her smile was bright and loving.

"Indeed, and a good thing too, for I could not have borne another day away from you, my dear." Again, I had the strangest sensation that while Father said one thing with his words, his voice held warning and worry.

Further explanation waited until he had dismounted and returned with us inside, removed his muddy garments, and joined us in mother's sitting room.

"The king felt he had kept me from my family far too much for far too long and granted me a leave," he said. His expression shifted slightly. "He said I had earned it for a job well done with this last raid."

Mother shot Father a warning look, but he shook his head. "No, Mariann. It is best that Henry, and even Madelin, should begin to know. We raided the Lanzenbergs. The king found evidence of treason, plotting to assassinate him and take the throne themselves."

"But the Lanzenbergs are a powerful family!" Mother exclaimed. "They've held the land for five hundred years—and that's a hundred years longer than the king's family has ruled! They're a good family. I cannot believe them traitors."

My father regarded her steadily, and though I knew there was some kind of unspoken communication between them, I was too young to know the language of life, love, and experience that they used.

Finally, Father said evenly, "The king thinks they are traitors, and that is all that matters."

"How long before he thinks such of any whose shadow grows as long as his?" Mother demanded.

"That is the kind of talk that makes him look twice at any shadow," he said grimly. "We must show our loyalty to the king now more than ever. Every word we speak, even to each other, must be nothing but perfection in our devotion to his majesty. That includes the children. Our allegiance is all that protects us."

Madelin glanced at me, her small, pretty face a picture of puzzlement. I nodded gravely to emphasize Father's words, though I didn't fully understand them myself. But, if loyalty was what he wished of me, then I would give it with my whole heart.

The next morning, the servants whispered among themselves how the lord and lady had spent half the night in conference. The bread and sun rose according to schedule, and the bailiff of my father's estates met with him, just as my mother directed the affairs of the house. Yet, something was different. The strings of the lacings of our family life had been pulled tight by an unseen hand.

That night, we sat before the hearth in Father's study. Mother worked on hemming swaddling cloths for our tenants, and Madelin drowsed snuggled up against her. I worked my way through dry Latin grammar, glancing surreptitiously at Father's knotted face as he reviewed the estate books.

"T'understorm," Madelin mumbled sleepily.

I strained to hear the thunder, but the look Mother and Father shared told me they feared the approach of a different storm.

The rumble of horses riding up to the house carried the wind, the clanging of armor audible as the group approached. I ran to the window and peeked through the shutters. There had to be at least twelve horsemen, all wearing silver armor that glistened in the light of twelve torches. The rider at the head of the party wore golden armor and a red cape.

Father stood, his face white.

"Mariann, take the children to the passages," he ordered quietly.

"What does he want, Frederick?" Mother asked. "You know what the king wants. Why is he here?"

"Now, Mariann!" Father roared.

There was only time for one more long, searching look between them, and then Mother was pushing me and dragging Madelin out the door and down the corridor to her bedchambers. Once inside, she ripped aside the hanging from behind her high wooden bed. Behind the headboard, the stones were set in a slightly different pattern. She pressed a carved rose on the headboard, and the stones swung open like a door, revealing a dark passage beyond.

"Henry, you go first," Mother panted. "I will hand Madelin to you."

I slithered over the headboard and landed lightly on the other side, reaching out to take hold of my sister. There was a banging at the door, and the wood snapped and groaned from the assault.

I froze and stared in horror at my mother's white face as her eyes filled with tears. The door splintered, and she pressed the wooden rose again.

"Run, Henry," she whispered. "Run."

The last I saw of my mother and sister were their terrified eyes as the stone door slammed shut between us. The darkness closed in around me, and my body found the will to move again. I raised my fists to beat against the stones. I could hear her voice, loud and calm, though the words were muffled by rock. I heard the guards yell out, and Madelin screamed.

Frantically, I felt for the outline of the door in the stones, but fear made my fingers clumsy. If I wanted to save my mother and Madelin, the only way I could reach them was by going forward.

And so, into the darkness I plunged.

The passage was narrow and nasty, but I paid no heed to the scrapes on my skin or the dizzying stench. In a numb haze of dread, I pushed ahead. I felt the jab of a corner against my shoulder, and on turning it, I saw a tiny pinhole of light ahead. I rushed toward it, crushed that it was not an exit, only a spyhole.

I heard the sound of voices from the other side of the wall, and I pressed my eye to the hole. At the very least, I might find out what part of the castle I was in and have a better idea of how to escape these tunnels. My heart dropped into the pit of my stomach at what I saw.

"Fine land, you have here, cousin," King Edward said, seating himself at my father's desk and throwing his boots up on the table, careless of the papers he sullied. "Very fine. Your family has been treated well by mine."

"Yes, quite well," my father replied cautiously. "Our lines have always thrived on our mutual respect and trust."

The king smirked. I had not realized how young the king was. True, he was ten years older than I, but his face was still youthful—or it would have been if not for the cruelty that dug deep lines about his eyes. "Trust. Yes, a rare commodity these days. I am grateful I have at least one ally."

Father's shoulders relaxed slightly, but not enough.

The king picked up a porcelain figurine off the desk. It was a brightly painted shepherd, a small herd of frozen sheep surrounding its feet. He inspected the statuette lovingly, running his fingers over the smooth surface.

"Worth anything?" he asked, changing the subject. He turned the figure over, looking at the base for any sign of a mark.

"I'm not sure," my father replied. "I would imagine it would have some value. It was a gift from your grandfather to my own."

"Ah!" he said, eyes narrowing. "How decent of him."

He held it out with a straight arm and slowly unwrapped his fingers from around the shepherd's neck until it inevitably fell to the floor. I jumped as the crash rumbled through the ground, the figurine exploding into thousands of colorful shards.

My father was a braver man than I, though. He stood his ground, not even flinching. His gaze hardened, and I imagined it was the look upon his face he wore into battle.

"Why are you here, your majesty?" he asked grimly, as if he already knew the answer.

The king jumped to his feet and slammed his fists down on the desk. "Don't play me for a fool! You know very well why!"

"Then say it...cousin."

King Edward kicked the glass head of the shepherd across the floor and spat, "Treason!"

"Prove it." It was as if I was watching flame beat upon rock, terror upon gravity.

The king stalked over to stand directly before my father. He had to tilt his chin up ever so slightly in order to look my father in the eye.

"Your very existence is proof enough...cousin," he said, his mouth twisting sourly on the last word.

"My existence?" Father repeated calmly.

"Blood." The syllables dripped from the king's lips. "You and I share the same blood, blood that gives you the right to my throne."

"I don't want your throne," Father said coldly.

"See? Treason! You speak as though you could ever have it, could ever take it from me! Treason runs in your blood." The king whipped a dagger from his belt and unceremoniously thrust it into my father's neck. "And now, your blood will run for your treason."

I looked at my father's shocked face, feeling abstracted from any real emotion as I watched dark, gloppy blood spurt from his neck with each pulse of his fading heart. The king had just stabbed my father. I knew that fact, but it seemed more the artifact of some nightmare, soon to be dispelled.

King Edward swallowed hard, and his hand on the blade shook. I wondered if he had ever actually dealt a death blow before. How strange that my father should be the first.

"The shame of it all is that I was quite fond of you," he said, swallowing convulsively again as he yanked the knife from my father's throat and kicked him in the chest, sending him crashing back to the floor. "If only you were as loyal as you claimed, I would never have had to do this. But then, if you are as loyal as you claim, then you will understand why I had to."

I rolled the words around my head, trying to make sense of them. But, it is futile to try and make a madman sensible. A man who plungers a dagger into the heart of a dying man is not one who sets any great store by logic.

Panic began to trickle back in as I watched my father begin to choke and convulse, his eyes rolling back in his head. The blood seeped from his chest and joined the dark pool behind his head. But, even this slowed and stopped.

"I am truly sorry it had to end this way," the king said. The sincerity in his voice drove me to retch silently as not even the sight of my father's blood could. "Goodbye, cousin."

He pulled the knife from Father's chest, which now lay unnaturally still. I held my own breath, waiting for it to rise again. The king put an end to my hopes by lifting his boot and stomping down on Father's heart. There was a crack of ribs, a final small gush of blood, and it was done.

"Thomas!" the king called out.

He wiped the dagger on the curtains. The door of the study whipped open. A guard rushed in, paying no attention to my father's lifeless body. Everything spun around me as hot tears welled in my eyes. This was real. Happening. Time was truly moving forward without my father.

"Yes, your majesty?"

"Lock them all in. I don't want anyone getting out."

"The children, too?"

The king shot him a look of death. "Are you questioning me? I hope not, or your usefulness to me will grow thin."

"Of course not, your majesty," he choked in reply.

"Good. Once we are finished here I want you to send out an edict immediately," the king said. "The name Rumpelstiltskin is no longer welcome in our kingdom. It is a cursed name. It shall be struck from every document and every history. I want everyone in our kingdom to know what I do to traitors."

"Yes, your highness," the guard replied.

My breath stopped.

"Now go. I don't want to waste another moment in this bloody house. Though it is a shame to destroy something so fine. That wife of his is rather pretty."

The guard left and I heard a rush of armored men racing up the stairs followed by a chorus of locking doors. My mother's and sister's cries echoed down.

The king walked over to the table and picked up a candelabra, quickly lighting every wick. He watched eagerly as the flames flickered to life. With a flourish, he took the burning candles and set them against the curtains. A wicked smile pulled on his lips as he ignited anything in reach. Fire licked up the heavy fabrics. The wood paneling blistered. Loud crackles and snaps feasted on the house as it was engulfed in an inferno. He left, taking the candles with him, setting more blazes throughout the house. The screams resonated down and stung my ears. I had to save my mother and sister.

Thick smoke already wafted into the passageway as I crawled through the dark. I had to find my way out so I could find my way back in. My lungs wheezed and the blaze grew along with their frantic cries.

My eyes burnt with ash.

"I'm coming!" I shouted, coughing up smoke.

The roll of flame and smoke blocked several turns, but finally, I found something made of wood and not stone. A door. I pushed at the locks and yanked the handle with all my might until I finally stumbled out into a corridor. I didn't know where I was. Flames surrounded me, stinging my skin with heat. Smoke blinded me and turned every wall into a stranger.

There were so many screams now. I tried to tell which cries of agony belonged to my mother and Madelin, but I quickly learned that the sounds of death by burning are all alike.

I was hopelessly turned around and growing weak from smoke and terror. A metallic hand reached for me out of the smoke and grasped my shoulder in an unforgiving grip.

"No!" I choked, scrabbling at the disembodied hand. "Let go! I have...to...save them!"

But the hand didn't listen and only pulled harder, dragging me away. Orange flames flickered through the gray smoke. My feet kicked and hands flailed.

"No!" I screamed, learning quickly that the sounds of survival could be worse than those of death.

It was too late. The soot cleared from my vision, and I saw I was no longer in the house at all, but outside, lying on the parched ground beneath the smoky moon.

"Hush, or we'll both be back in that inferno!" a voice snapped above me.

I looked up and was shocked to see it was the same guard I had seen moments ago. The one who had ignored my father. Thomas.

"You're safe now," he said, doubled over and hacking up the ash from his lungs.

I struggled up to my feet, only to be pushed back down.

"It's too late!" he snarled. "They're already dead. You're lucky I could save you."

"No they aren't! There is time. I can still hear them scream!" I yelled.

His expression shifted. "It's only a memory," he said quietly. "They are long gone."

Behind him, fire painted the house in broad strokes of orange and crimson. Walls crumbled and fell. The roof collapsed with a great roll and wave of sparks and cinders. I stared helplessly as everything I had known disintegrated to ash. My body trembled as each glowing ember sailing up to heaven was a soul that I had known and loved, their lights winking out and leaving me alone.

Finally, rage found its way to me. I jumped once more to my feet and charged Thomas, throwing my fists with force but no skill.

"Why did you save me? You should have let me die. At least I could have been with my family."

He caught my hands easily and once more threw me down, only this time, he knelt down, pressing one knee into my chest to make his point. Stay down.

I registered soot-stained skin and ash-lined wrinkles. But, it was his startling blue eyes that held me more firmly than his hands ever could.

"I couldn't stand idly by and watch your destiny be destroyed," he panted.

There were two of him now. No, three. Three sets of blue eyes staring at me. I gulped down air that my lungs refused, coughing until I was dizzy. Three sets of white teeth smiling reassuringly.

"Destiny?" I repeated. It wasn't my destiny that mattered. It was my father, mother, sister, servants, home, and friends that had been brutally burned to death.

"I'm afraid there isn't time to have a philosophical discussion. Right or wrong, the king has marked you a traitor, my boy. Killed your family and taken away your birthright. For now, your destiny must be to run."

He stood and took out his sword, pointing it over my heart. The glimmer in his eyes turned vicious, and his smile vanished. "Run, boy. I've saved your life once, but I won't again. The wilderness is your home now. Go and claim your new kingdom."

The sharp blade poked into my chest and I had no choice but to take several steps backward. Fear gripped my throat, and my already muddled mind blurred any hope of comprehension of what was happening. All I could do was obey.

"Run!" he commanded again.

Head pounding, I focused all my energy on my legs and ran into the forest. Trees curved, and the ground bled into the sky, but I continued to run through the mist overtaking my head. Hallucinations nipped at my heels, and my lungs begged for air and rest, but still I kept running.

For the first time in my life, I was utterly alone. I became a child lost to the wilderness, left with nothing but twisted memories and a pain so putrid and festering, it would eventually consume me.

CHAPTER NINE

Yarn:

noun: spun thread used for knitting, weaving, or sewing.

verb: tell a long or implausible story

AFTER ALL: RUMPELSTILTSKIN

The castle was full of light, within, without, and above from torches, candles, and fireworks. The rhythm of drums and shrill notes of recorders tumbled through the night air.

This was the celebration of an era. A ball held in honor of the newest addition to the king's heart and I, the uninvited guest, was about to crash it. Chills rolled down my spine just thinking of my hand strangling his joy until it was nothing but a purple carcass.

Getting past the guards was stupidly easy. Nothing more than a glamour and an imperious nod, and I in. The major domo was a bit more of a challenge. Those whose lives and minds revolve around rules are always a bit harder to fool, but fools will be fooled, rules or not. It only required a small bit of magic to tweak his will to announcing me as "Ambassador Fortuna," as it was not really a lie. After all, I was to be the herald of the king's destiny...and the queen's. I ruthlessly suppressed the queer pang in my chest at the thought of her and went ahead.

The great hall was nothing short of a Venetian hell, a farce of a morality play with leering Harlequins, flirtatious feathered lace that hardly hid anything at all, and the roiling aroma of heavy perfumes, incense, and roast meat.

What sickened me more than the outward display were the inward flames of desperate souls glowing around me. Brightly they burned, each wanting more than the blessings they already were given.

More gold. More beauty. More pleasure, their voices whispered in my ears, until I heard little else. *More. More. MORE.*

I stalked out onto the terrace to breathe cleaner air and clear my head from the siren calls of the starving. I was there for business this evening, not pleasure...though in the end, my business would be my pleasure. I would finally look into Laila's eyes and—

No. What? No, my true pleasure would be looking into the king's eyes and watching the unquenchable flames of his greedy soul wilt and die. The queen mattered nothing at all. She was just a pawn. Nothing more.

Said pawn was currently sitting on a throne of gold, wearing a gown of purple silk embroidered with—guess what—gold thread. Squinting, I looked closer and saw that the pattern of the embroidery was made up entirely of wheels with spokes. The spinning queen. How fitting. I wondered what her newly royal family coat of arms would be? A spinning wheel on a golden field, perhaps with crossed quills? The notion tickled my fancy, and with a sardonic smile on my lips, I crossed the crowd to her.

As I drew closer, I noticed the changes that a year had wrought. Her skin was paler, thanks to parasols and velvet canopies. Her chestnut hair cascaded down her shoulders, and I wondered if she still smelled of citrus and rose oil. Her eyes still flashed fiercely at everything around them, though the circles underneath them revealed the efforts of childbirth and sleepless nights after. My eyes slid down her neck, and I froze, my cock stirring and making walking uncomfortable. Motherhood had endowed her natural abundance with even more...abundance.

Skin on straw...hot, harsh breaths...hands on velvet, on hair, on lips...

I shook away the heat. I had business of a different sort to attend to tonight. Perhaps when this was all done and in the long dead past...

Laila immediately stiffened as I came before her and bowed. For the first time since all those nights ago, her eyes met mine. Power flourished and pumped through my veins as her expression betrayed the smallest flash of fear, but a disappointing mask of cool resolve quickly hid it away.

"Enjoying the party?" I smirked. "I must compliment your *majesty* on the unnecessarily lavish display."

"You are not welcome here." Ooh, my Laila was attempting to freeze me with grand royal contempt. I resisted the impulse to clap.

"I am under no illusions, madam. I never expected you to receive me...with open arms." Perhaps my allusion to our momentary mésalliance was wrong of me, seeing as how I tasted something bitter when she blanched and blushed, but it was done.

"Why have you chosen to come on this particular night?" she asked, the first crack in the royal mask slowly showing.

"Let us just say that I am never one to let a *golden* opportunity pass me by. Besides, I am not in the wrong here. If I'm not mistaken it is you who are beholden to me. I can appear whenever and wherever I wish."

Her eyes flashed, and her lips grew quite thin. She was pretty when she was angry, which was most of the time. I wondered if I provoked her just to see the heated rise and fall of her chest.

Again I bowed before her, adding extra flourish to the way I extended my hand. "Lest you think I am all pride, I beg—indeed, most fervently—for the privilege of a dance with your majesty."

She stared at my hand as if I held the very plague in my palm. "You cannot be serious," she said through clenched teeth. "Why would I ever accept such an invitation from you?"

"Because, madam, people are beginning to notice you talking to an exceptionally handsome and dashing, though sadly unknown, fellow. There are no rules against conversing while dancing, but to speak as intently as we are, well... I would take my hand, if I were you, before they get too nosey and their gossip makes it to the king's ears. We must keep up appearances if we wish to discuss the matter further."

I ignored the flash of hurt at the look of resignation in her eyes as she rose and placed her hand in mine.

"If you hadn't chosen to come to the ball," she said quietly, now through a bland smile. "We would have been concerned for our appearances."

Ah, my clever girl. "I would be happy to oblige your majesty next time by appearing in your bedroom in the dead of night for any further intimate conversations."

"Straw is not all that you spin," she said, still smiling perfectly, though unable to hide the slight rolling of her eyes.

I was delighted with her progress from miller's daughter to queen. Her caustic wit was still very much in evidence, but it had been refined and sharpened by exposure to the witty repartee of court. Her movements through the opening of the dance were a graceful world away from the weary scurrying across a dungeon floor to fill baskets of straw. She was simply magnificent, and I felt comforted in the thought that after the king's coming 'decline,' she would be the kind of monarch the kingdom needed.

In the next turn of the dance, I placed my hand on the small of her back and pulled her against me. The feel of her body on mine wrapped me in warm velvet, and I could see nothing but the nervous breath upon her lips.

"I know you've come for the child," she stated as the cry of the violins compelled our every move.

"I thought that rather obvious," I replied. Lifting her arm, I walked around her in a tight circle before pulling her roughly to me once again.

We glared at each other, feeling the pounding of each other's hearts. There was no escaping one another now. All one could do was push forward.

"There is a problem you did not foresee," she said, spinning in my arms and slipping one of her feet between mine to prepare for the next move. "I've changed my mind and you can't have him."

She stepped forward, and the dance obliged me to step back. Oh, what a mastery of irony she had acquired. I tightened my grip around her waist and picked her up to spin her around once before setting her down. I pulled her with me as I stepped back, compelling her to move forward in a parody of leading.

"That is a shame," I said. "It could have been so easy for you, but it looks like you've made the mistake of letting your heart get attached to what it knows it cannot have."

Her breaths grew quicker as on the next lift and spin, she repeated my movement and pulled me two steps back with her. I closed my eyes, unexpectedly caught by a vision of her roughly pushing me back onto my back as she climbed upon me and...

I released her and circled her as I had at the beginning, the steps beginning all over again.

Once more, I yanked her in, carelessly allowing myself to revel in the feel of her breasts and hips pressing against me.

"Why don't you just be a good girl, fetch the child, and we can get this nasty business all over with," I said, lowering my head to whisper in her ear, letting my lips brush the delicate flesh. "Then you can move on with the rest of your life."

"No," she responded, turning her face so that our lips were no more than a breath apart. "You don't understand. I *won't* let you take him. I will fight for him until you bleed."

"I'd be careful if I were you," I hissed. "Breaking a deal with me is not so simple as you might think. You gave me your name. Signed it away in your own blood with these sweet fingers of yours." I raised her fingers to my lips and kissed the tip of one, daring to give it the barest suckle. "If you break our agreement, nothing but darkness awaits your soul."

She gasped, and for a moment, I was confused whether her reaction was that of fear or desire, or perhaps both. Or was it my own reaction of fear and desire that had shaken me? The thought of Laila taken by the darkness that awaited oath-breakers was suddenly and utterly intolerable.

A shadow fell upon us.

"How dare you be so familiar with my queen!"

I froze at the sound of that voice. I saw blood, smelled smoke, and heard the screams of the dying. Blinking I was back in the ballroom, looking upon gold, smelling perfumed oil, and listening to the sound of violins.

Still holding his queen in my arms, I turned to see King Edward for the first time since I was a boy. He looked much older than last I saw him, but that was to be expected. Lean muscle and sharp angles now replaced the gangly youth, but that couldn't hide the monster he was. I wanted to rip out his throat, but he didn't deserve such a kindness.

"Who the bloody hell are you?" he bellowed, ripping Laila from my arms and forcing her to his side.

The dancers stopped, and the chatter died away, along with the flutes and the drums. All eyes were on us. The last note of a violin died away in the silence.

"That depends on who you ask," I replied, pleased that my voice did not shake from rage. "To some, I am a savior, and to others, a nightmare. To you, I am judgment."

He laughed heartily. A few nervous chuckles rose from the crowd, following their monarch's example.

"Only an ass would hide behind a riddle," the king retorted.

"Only a fool would not be able to solve it," I countered with the ease of catching a ball clumsily thrown by a child.

The laughter dissolved into gasps. The king's amusement ended at his lips.

"Kill him," he spat to his guards.

Flashes of rattling silver and steel came at me from both sides.

"I take it we are not in a playful mood this evening?" I taunted. "Good. Neither am I."

I twisted my wrists, and the guard's necks snapped like twigs. Their bodies fell to the floor with a brassy clatter. The king stared blankly at the dead men with his mouth open, like some dumb animal.

"I think you might want to reconsider listening to what I have to say, Eddy—may I call you Eddy? We have a considerable amount of business to get through tonight," I stated.

The room shuddered at the sound of my voice, and I loved the sensation. King Edward tilted his head to the side as if trying to understand exactly who...or what...stood before him.

"What do you want?" he asked.

"Nothing but the debt I am owed."

Confusion flooded his expression. "What on earth would that be?"

"Your firstborn," I replied casually.

The king let out a nervous chuckle. I could see he wanted to believe I was simply mad.

"I am afraid you are mistaken in my identity," he said in a voice reserved only for fools and children. "I have never contracted any debt with you."

"Quite right," I agreed. "But she has," I added, gesturing to Laila. "I take it she never told you about our little agreement?"

The king glared at Laila. An awful silence fell on the crowd until Laila spun to face them.

"Leave us, all of you," she commanded. "For God's sake, get out!"

The floor shook as the revelers stampeded towards the door. Goblets and plates fell like golden hail on the ground as the courtiers escaped into the safety of the night.

"Too bad." I clucked my tongue. "I feel I always perform better before an audience."

Laila shot me a look of disgust. It was just like old times.

"You cutthroat bitch!" the king spat, turning on Laila and backhanding her. The blow spun her, and my fingers twitched with the need to teach him a lesson about throat-cutting, then and there.

Holding her cheek, Laila straightened up to her full height, her eyes bright with hate for both of us.

"I hardly think Laila deserves all the blame in this little mess," I said, cutting off her comments for her own safety. The king's attention swung back to me, and I saw the small, savory flame of desperation beginning to pulse in his soul. "If I recall, it was only because of you that she was driven to make such a deal in the first place. What kind of fool believes a drunk when he says his daughter can spin straw into gold? Wait, do not answer. I think I know. It must be a king whose greed for gold and power far outstrips his feeble powers of reasoning. Wouldn't you agree?"

During my speech, I had sauntered over to the thrones and casually dropped myself into the king's seat. He saw naught but lese majesté, but I took a moment to think of my father and of the boy I was, the boy who could have been but never wanted to be king.

"So, what is a poor girl to do when the big, bad, mad king threatens —most convincingly—to cut off her head when she can't perform the impossible?" I continued, nonchalantly waving my fingers and conjuring a piece of straw to twirl lazily in the air. "Can you fault her for seizing the opportunity to save herself?"

A slight twist of my fingers, and the straw began to gleam with the brilliance of gold. It was almost laughable the way the king's eyes went wide at the sight. Almost.

"All those nights she spent locked away in that dungeon, I was there spinning for her. Every thread you worship ran through my fingers."

His face turned a nasty shade of purple as he trembled.

"What is your proof of such an arrangement?" he seethed. "I demand to see the contract."

"Very wise," I chuckled. Bringing my hands together in a clap that echoed like thunder. "I am more than happy to grant such a request."

Standing from the throne, I opened my palm and the contract appeared, the scroll unwinding itself as it rolled to the floor and all the way to the king's feet. He looked at the bottom of the paper, and the purple infecting his face dissolved into white. Laila's name still gleamed in her own blood as fresh as the day she first signed.

AFTER ALL: LAILA

I **looked upon** my folly, committed by my own hand. I tried to unravel the tangle of events in my mind, to see if there had been a moment when I could have chosen differently. Yet, without the exact choices I had made, Tristan would never have been born.

Love and pain warred in my heart, but they were nothing to the clarion call of motherhood that demanded that I give nothing less than my all to protect my child now.

"Is it true?" Edward demanded. "Did you commit this treason?"

"Yes," I answered with a shrug. What was the point of denying the truth?

"*Yes*?" he roared. "That's it? That's all you have to say?"

"What more is there to say?" I shot back. "I saw no other way out except the offer he made me of my life, a good life, and I grasped it tight in my fist. Was I just supposed to let myself die at your hands when there was a chance I could live?"

Explaining actual human emotion, fear, to Edward was futile. He remained unmoved, incapable, the contract proving my sin clutched in his hand. I looked back to the stranger, the man who stood between my child and me. He looked wild, hungry, like some beast roving through a wood. I knew he could tear me limb from limb, but I would not succumb without a fight.

I stood before the stranger. He glared at me, and I remembered how he had detested my weakness. Now, I realized that he hated my weakness because he must have been vulnerable to it somehow. Perhaps it reminded him of his own feelings which he tried so hard to repress. Pain was power, yes, but I also knew that weakness could be strength. I hated I had to permit that pleading side of me I wished to forget to bleed through once again, but I had no choice.

"You're going to rip away an innocent child from its mother just because I was scared? Because I wanted to live?" I asked, allowing the horror of it all to swell deep within my heart. For the first time, he remained silent, and I took my chance to push my emotions harder, to let the raw anger flowing within my veins to roll down my cheeks and redden my eyes. "You just admitted I wasn't entirely to blame. I was backed into a corner. Trapped. You gave me my only chance. I'm asking you now, here, for another chance. Just one more, and then you can do what you will."

His muscles stiffened. Tears fell from my eyes, and I let them roll down my face. I wanted him to see my torment, to aggravate him into understanding my rage.

It did not take long before I noticed his right eye twitching, his lips moving hungrily as he placed his hand over my heart. He let his fingers graze my skin, and I cursed myself as my stomach coiled from his touch as it never had for Edward. His gaze fell to where he continued to caress my skin, his eyes intense and nearly smoldering. Then, he pressed his hand firmly to my chest, as if desperately trying to retrieve some treasure he frantically wanted.

"Just one chance. That's all I ask." I pushed again, a fresh wave of pain rolling through me.

He pulled back his hand as if burned.

"Stop!" he groaned, turning away. "Always tears! You are giving me an awful headache with your blubbering." He gave a small sigh before letting his attention fall back to the king. "I seem to be in a rather generous spirit today. Laila has asked for a chance, and so a chance is what I will give you."

"Out with it!" Edward snapped.

"Three days," he said quietly. "I will give you three more precious days with your child, and if in that time you can guess my name, you can keep the little beast. But if you fail, then the child remains mine."

My heart leapt.

"Your name? That's it?" Edward asked.

The stranger ignored him, concentrating instead on a new scroll taking shape in his hand. Those same cryptic symbols covered every inch of the paper. The king snatched the parchment and inspected the miniscule scratches.

"I just have to guess your name and you'll leave us in peace?" Edward asked again.

"Yes," the stranger replied. "All you have to do is sign, and so it shall be."

A black quill appeared between his long fingers, the same quill he had presented to me. I felt chilled at the memory of its bite on my fingertips.

"Don't worry about ink," he said as he handed it to Edward.

"No!" I cried.

Both men looked at me, confused, as I snatched the quill away from Edward's hand. Rage burned in Edward's eyes, but I didn't care. I couldn't allow the same mistake to happen twice. This had to be thought through. I didn't want another deal. I wanted freedom.

"Making a new deal will only enslave us further. He wouldn't make something so easy if it weren't for his own gain. "

"Shut up!" Edward roared. "You've nearly destroyed everything. Do you really want to finish the job?"

He seized my arm and ripped the quill out of my grasp. The tip of the instrument scraped across my hand, leaving searing pain in its wake. My blood welled up from the wound, and I stared at it, desperately trying to think through all the moves of this maniac's deadly game of chess.

"My patience is growing thin." The stranger's words were uncommonly cold. His eyes remained transfixed on the sticky red liquid flowing down my fingers. "You either sign, or I take the child now."

The paper rustled in Edward's hand as if possessing a life of its own, and the quill responded with a quiver in his fingers, yearning for the bliss of the page. It did not have to wait long. The quill twisted and twirled across the parchment as the king carved his name into its welcoming embrace.

Red filled his face as he endured the pain I knew to be burning his fingertips. His hand remained firm, though, leaving a trail of bright red blood behind until it was finished. He gave a groan, throwing the quill to the floor once it was done and looked at his fingers.

"See, that wasn't so hard, was it?" the stranger asked, rolling up the contract. "I will see you in three days. Better enjoy your remaining moments with your son."

He gave one final grimace in my direction and, without any warning, vanished completely, leaving me alone with Edward.

CHAPTER TEN

AFTER ALL: KING EDWARD

"**What is his** name?" I shouted at the bitch. I know she was refusing to tell me for some twisted reason of her own. "WHAT'S HIS NAME?"

"I already told you, I don't know," she hissed back. She looked feral with her eyes narrowed and teeth bared. A wild bitch that I once thought I had tamed but who had turned on me and bitten my giving hand.

"How many more times must I tell you?" she continued. "He never told me. Not even a hint. Don't you think I would tell you if I knew? I want to save our child just as much as you."

"Don't presume to tell me what to think!" I roared back. "Why should I believe someone capable of selling my child to a demon?"

She groaned in frustration. "We are wasting time arguing. Let me go out and search. I have the best chance. I already got him to give us three days, and I know I could get him to free us from this debt entirely."

She must have been truly mad to think I'd allow such a thing. "You aren't going anywhere."

"Why not?"

I glared at her and pressed my finger over her lying lips.

"Because I don't trust you," I said. "You lost my trust the moment you signed my son away. I should've killed you when I had the chance."

She knocked my hand away and strode the length of our chambers before turning back to me and spitting, "What a pity to have missed your chance. If only you hadn't been so afraid of your precious gold turning into ash."

She played with fire now, and my fingers curled, hungering for her neck.

My son started to cry, and his mournful wails tolled in my ears. Trying to gain control of my anger, I walked towards the cradle and caressed one of his plump cheeks. A faint rose blushed over his milky skin as he finally quieted down. Warmth I rarely knew washed over me as I comforted him. He wasn't just the protection I always craved for my power, he was my child, and I wanted his love.

"Nothing will happen to you, my son. The only one who will pay for this sin is that whore," I whispered to him as I stroked his hair.

As if he could hear my murderous thoughts, his little face scrunched with anger. For a moment, and maybe it was a trick of the flickering candlelight, his green eyes locked onto mine in a pointed glare that seemed to scream: *Don't kill her! I will never forgive you for killing my mother!*

I saw utter hatred in my son's gaze. My throat clamped shut, seized by the fear my son might loathe me forever. But his mother deserved punishment.

Don't kill her! I will never forgive you and I will despise you for making me motherless. Tristan's eyes begged, his fear and grief piercing my heart.

I picked him up and cradled him to my chest. When I held him after he was born, I saw a prize, a possession. Now, for the first time, though I had always called him *my* son, I felt like *his* father. He trusted me, not as his sovereign, but as his flesh and blood. To protect him was now the consuming passion that ran through my veins.

"Sire!"

I turned to see Captain Rowan stumbling into the room, his hand pressed to his chest as he panted. The man must have run all the way from the armory.

"The first search party has just returned," he gasped out. "Unfortunately, no name was discovered. There is no trace of him anywhere."

"Impossible!" I said. "I saw the man walk out of the ballroom with my own eyes. He couldn't have just vanished. Someone must have seen him leave the palace!"

I watched Rowan as small beads of sweat collected across his forehead before trickling down his temples. He was nervous. No...he was terrified.

"He is a ghost, sire," Rowan said, not meeting my gaze. Nobody has seen anything. Nobody knows anything."

I walked over to the fire and grabbed the poker. I prodded the logs, plumes of ash and sparks flying into the air.

"A ghost? I see." I repeated flatly.

Another cloud of embers billowed up as I shoved the poker deeper into the coals. A fresh wave of heat pressed against my skin.

"Do you know what I think, Rowan?" I asked.

"N-no, sire."

"I think you know something," I said. Lifting the hot poker from the flames, I admired its glowing red tip before I spun around and brought it within a hair's breadth of his cheek. "I think you know—just as I do—that this man is no ghost."

Rowan's eyes went wide with animal fear at the sight of the poker, and human fear twisted his mouth as my words sunk in.

"P-please, sire," he whispered.

"I have the oddest suspicion you are hiding something from me. I can always tell. Men like you tend to piss their pants when they keep secrets and sweat balls when they lie."

I touched the poker to his beard, breathing in the stink of burning hair.

"Edward, this is insane!" Laila cried, rushing at me and grabbing my arm.

I shook her off me, casting her to the floor.

"Shut up!" I snapped. "He is either going to tell me, or I am going to shove this poker through his cheek and burn off his tongue. You hear that, Rowan?"

Laila's eyes grew round with horror, yet, she didn't dare rise up again to oppose me. Rowan blanched, and I watched with pleasure as his soldierly stoicism collapsed along with his legs. I grabbed him by the collar, just as I would grab a dog by the scruff.

"You don't understand, sire," he whimpered. "I was sworn to secrecy. I'm bound by blood!"

Laila gasped, and I felt a prickling in my fingertips from where they held that damned demon's quill. I brought the poker back to Rowan's beard and singed the other side. The symmetry pleased me, as did his frantic jerking and squirming in my grasp.

"I-I've seen him before," Rowan cried out, his words tumbling forth. "Once. In a tavern, a year ago, before I was made captain of the guard."

"And?" I let the word hang in the air.

"S-sire?"

"Come now, Rowan. I thought you somewhat intelligent, but you must think me a fool if you believe I accept that's all that happened."

The man looked down, and I saw a tear roll down his cheek. Disgusting.

"He offered me everything," he whispered. "I couldn't refuse. I made a deal with him."

"What did he offer you?" Not that it mattered, but I had to break him by humiliation in order to be sure I got everything out of him.

"Everything...Evelyn...my position as captain...but, he made me promise not to tell a soul about our pact, or I would know the keenest torment."

I pondered this.

"What tavern?" I asked.

"The Red Lion, by the north gate of the city."

"Well, there's one thing that is certain," I said mildly, the poker still clutched in my fist.

"What, sire?"

"The man, unlike you, is not a liar. You will, in fact, know the keenest torment."

With that, I raised the poker and brought it down with all the force my rage could muster. Bone cracked and skin sizzled. Hot blood sprayed across my face and chest, but I didn't relent. I struck him again, his screams briefly filling the room until the metal rod crushed through his skull and he went silent. Brains and blood oozed out of the wound. Placing my foot on his disfigured face I pulled out the buried rod, white clumps sticking to the metal.

I turned back towards Laila, who had clapped both her hands over her mouth. I pointed the bloodied poker at her.

"Not a word, woman," I said. "And, for the love of God, if you're going to be sick, do it in the pot, not on the floor."

She crawled to the chamber pot, and I heard her casting up her accounts. I opened the door and bawled for a page.

"Your majesty?" the lad asked, bowing nervously as he entered the room.

"Prepare me clothing. Plain and poor like that which a commoner might wear."

"Sire?" The boy whispered, glancing between the body on the floor and my blood-spattered self.

"God's teeth! Am I condemned to be surrounded by liars and fools? What of my words did you not understand? Clothing. Plain. Dirty. Poor. NOW!"

He nearly tripped running out the door.

"What are you going to do?" Laila asked, cautiously rising to her feet.

"Since everyone seems to be either a numbwit or a fraud, I shall go find the man's name myself."

"Is that wise? What if you are discovered? What if you are killed? What of the kingdom then?"

"You have precious little faith in me, madam, though I've kept my word to you in all things."

"Let me go instead," Laila pushed. "You have never been a commoner, you do not know how to carry yourself or speak without giving yourself away. I know my way around these people."

I laughed bitterly. "You? Let you leave the palace? Trust *you*? Nay, you will stay here with my son. You can fill the hours by contemplating the gift I have given you of your life. Again. Yes, you are safe from the scaffold. I will not have a son raised without a mother. He'd never forgive me. Don't test my mercy further."

"You don't know the meaning of the word!" she said.

"Oh, but I do, my dear. I am going to fix this mistake of yours, and then we shall go on with our lives. I will have a son who loves me utterly and an obedient wife that will do everything I say."

"And, why do you think that?" she spat.

"Because tonight you've lost your power over me. If you step a foot out of line, say one word that displeases me, I might let the truth slip. I will tell our sweet boy that dear mummy sold him for a bit of sweet meats and fine dresses. I'm sure he will be very understanding."

Sometimes, it is not the hand that delivers the stunning blow, but rather the mouth. With these words, I watched her realize that everything was forfeit to me. She finally understood just how dangerous games like hers could be.

THE SMELL WAS the worst part of the miserable clothing I wore, but it was nothing compared to the stench of the city. I knew it was a merry prank for royal youths to dress as commoners and mingle with them, but I had never desired to do so.

What kind of company could be expected from people who spent every day scrounging for a bit of gruel only to die the moment the wind turned cold. In my more cynical moments, I hardly knew why they bothered living at all.

Near the north gate, the crowds seemed to grow thicker, and I had to push my way forward through the square. At one end stood a ramshackle stage where several actors performed a litany of lewd jokes, while at the other end, gamblers squatted on the cobblestones, their hoots and wails punctuating the performance.

Idiots.

Continuing on, I passed several old beggar women crouched motionless along the walls. They held their hands out from mountains of rags.

"A coin for a blessing, sir. No evil shall befall the generous," one croaked. She lifted a gnarled claw towards me, a map of veins throbbing through papery skin.

I was enraged at the flagrant lese majesté of the woman actually truing to touch me but remembered just in time that she was not supposed to know I was her king. I hurried away from her clutching hands.

Thankfully unhindered by any more beggars or whores, I entered The Red Lion. It was as I expected, except slightly less filled with shit.

"You gonna stand there all night or you gonna order something?" a barmaid snapped. "Haven't got all day."

"Ale," I said as I took a seat, trying not to betray my revulsion.

She left and quickly returned, plopping a large pint down in front of me. The froth slid down the mug, joining the sticky remnants of past ales on the table.

"Half a copper," she said.

Instead of the half copper she requested I pulled out a gold coin. Her eyes grew large seeing more treasure than she had ever earned in her entire putrid existence. Her demeanor instantly became friendly, and she trailed one of those dirty fingers down her neck.

"Just what are you expecting to get for that?" she asked in a horrifying simulacrum of flirtation.

"An answer to a question, that's all," I replied, forcing a grin.

She snatched the coin from my hand and shoved it deep down within her bosom.

"I knew you must be a funny sort of man when you walked in here. It's always the strangers that have the oddest requests," she replied. Taking the seat in front of me, she didn't care to wince as her elbows landed on the sticky table.

"I'm looking for a name. A very important name, of a man I heard frequented this..." I had to force the words, "fine establishment. He has pale skin and black hair. He's a unique fellow. You would remember him if you had seen him."

I noticed several men glancing over in my direction. No doubt their ears were burning from our conversation just as their eyes must have been burning from the glimpse of the gold I'd given the woman.

"I think I know the man yer lookin' for, but I'm afraid I don't know nothin' 'bout a name. Creepy bloke if ever I saw one, though. Looked like an angel and a devil all at once."

More glances. The prying simpletons.

"Did he speak with anyone?" I asked.

"Oh, yeah. Aldus was the last to speak with him. The man bought him drinks and even egged him on. Thank goodness someone was willing to listen to Aldus' boasting. Gave my ears a break."

I leaned in, barely a breath escaping my lungs. This was the type of information I'd been hoping for. "Where can I find this Aldus?"

Her face grew quite somber. "Oh, he's dead now. Kept on about spinning wheels and turning straw into gold, the wanker. Said it was his fault his daughter was taken by the king, but we all knew his tall tales so we didn't believe a word of it. Fact is, he couldn't handle the truth his daughter ran away from a waste of a father. Drank himself to death he did, found him hunched over, face first in a pool of rum. Sitting right where you are, in fact."

My blood ran cold. Aldus was Laila's father! I stood up quickly, wondering how deep that bastard demon's manipulations went, but my thoughts were cut short as a wobbling man walked right into me and vomited onto my cloak. I'd had my fill of this place.

"How dare you!" I roared at the man.

Forgetting myself, I threw him to the ground. The barmaid rushed to his side. The group of men who had been glaring at me earlier joined her and stood between us.

"I suggest you leave," one cautioned.

"We don't take very kindly to such behavior from strangers, especially ones that ask so many questions," another interjected, reaching for the knife at his side.

I'd seen my share of fights, and even war. If ever there was a moment to call a retreat, this was it. I was without protection and outnumbered. They were rabid and restless, just like the wolves waiting to devour me whole.

I backed away slowly then ran once I reached the door.

I cursed them all as I found myself once again wandering the maze of streets, fearing my final chance at discovering the imp's name was lost.

I WALKED through the darkness for what seemed an eternity, asking passing strangers if they heard any murmurs of the name of the man I sought.

"Face like I never seen before. Don't quite reckon a name to go with it, I'm afraid," they all would say, my pouch lightening with every eager palm.

I decided to broaden my search and passed through the north gate and began to canvass the beggars and peddlers who camped outside the city walls. The death of my hope grew more certain with every step and every dead end, but was I not the king? Nothing was supposed to be outside my power to accomplish.

Darkness fell, and the bells tolled midnight, and then the hour past midnight. I skirted the edges of the woods that surrounded the city. I searched for hermits and woodsmen, but I soon realized my only remaining subjects in the forest were but foxes and rabbits.

Just as I was about to turn and leave the woods, a gust of wind bore down on me. The leaves rustled loudly, sounding like a chorus of whispers, but behind them were faintest notes of music.

My heart jumped a beat. The music grew clearer and stronger, and the melody yearned with the strings of a violin. Up and down the tune flew in hypnotic rhythms, its pulse beseeching me to follow.

Come, come this way!

Through the darkness I could make out the warm hues of a fire. The light ate away at the gloom revealing the mysterious violinist.

"Welcome, your majesty!" he said, never losing tempo as he continued to play. "I've been wondering when you'd come."

Swallowing my shock, I stepped out into the light. My shadow joined the others in their dance as he played a fresh set of scales and arpeggios.

"You look older than last I saw you. Yes. No longer a youth with spots on your skin."

"How do you know who I am?" I asked, shaken.

"Why, I know a great many people, sire, even though they never seem to notice me. But, you aren't here to ask such unimportant questions. No. You want to know the name of the man who is trying to steal your son."

The bow jumped and lilted over the strings and the melody changed as he began to sing, his strange blue eyes too bright, almost glowing.

I know the name you seek, and when you find out I'm sure you'll freak!

Dear King, think long and hard on your past, and remember the boy you left outcast.

Never will the king win this guessing game, so long as Rumpelstilt-skin is his name!

The weight of all my fears slammed me down to my knees.

"Rumpelstiltskin? Are you sure? How is that possible?" I whispered.

The flames of the fire jumped up to the sky, and when they died down, they revealed the man to be gone.

Rumpelstiltskin.

I killed my traitorous cousin and his entire family years ago. There was nothing left of the house. I made sure that accursed name was struck from every history I could find. This had to be a mistake. A joke.

Think long and hard on your past, and remember the boy you left outcast

Boy? I thought back to that day. There had been a wife and two children. I believe one of them was a son. Yes, that's right. I suppose it is possible he escaped. Could this stranger really be that boy, come back to punish me? To avenge his family? I thought several moments in the silence, only the crackle of the flames disrupting the quiet still. Then I started to laugh, feeling nearly mad with relief and rage.

"It is him! The traitor's boy has come back to seek vengeance on the king? How awfully clever!"

I nodded to my shadow, the dark figure applauding my victory. Even the fire seemed to congratulate me. The flames licked wickedly as they sent sparks flying into the air with every pop.

I knew his name, and I had nothing more to fear. The last Rumpel-stiltskin would die for his treason, just as he should have all those years ago.

CHAPTER ELEVEN

Thread:

verb: pass a thread through the eye of (a needle) or through the needle and guides of (a sewing machine).

verb: move carefully or skillfully in and out of obstacles.

UNHAPPILY: RUMPELSTILTSKIN

I **watched the** sun begin to sink, and I luxuriated in imagining the king in the castle, prey to the most sickening worry for his brat.

If I closed my eyes, I could see him, fingers drumming against his chair, anxiety bleeding through every cavity of his heart, sweat beading on his forehead until it rolled down his neck. I drifted pleasantly through these images, then a sharp summons voice cut through my peace like an ax through butter.

Come to me!

The king along with his delicious fear dissolved, and I was left with nothing but Laila's voice scraping in my head.

Come!

Vicious pain spread across my brain. I fought to block it. No one had ever summoned me like this before, but then again, no one had ever bound *my* blood to them in a contract. No doubt, that's how Laila found this channel through to me.

COME!

The veins in my temple throbbed, and my skull wanted to crack from the pressure. The agony was unrelenting, merciless, and I feared if I did not answer her fraught cries, my head would undoubtedly split in two.

What a lovely visit this promised to be.

Clenching my teeth to dull the pain, I closed my eyes and willed myself to go to her. I focused on the familiar despairing flame blazing in her chest I wished I didn't want so badly. In an instant, my room's wooden floorboards turned into palatial stone beneath my feet. The kiss of a burning fire heated my skin.

Opening my eyes, I saw Laila standing regally in the center of her private salon. There was a look of grim determination on her face. I sighed, partly because I didn't want to fight her, and partly because I wanted to kiss her frown away. Neither was a good option. The sooner I could get this fiasco of a visit over with the better.

"It takes courage to summon me here. Especially tonight," I hissed.

"I'm not afraid of you," she replied, every inch of her glorious form radiating queenly dignity and strength.

"You should be. I do not take kindly to house calls," I growled. "What's so important you dragged me up here? Are you going to appeal to my humanity again?"

"No."

"Really?" I asked, suddenly suspicious. The Laila I knew and understood would have rushed at me, begging and full of rage. This icy queen was an unknown player in my little chess game, and I had to be on my guard now more than ever.

"Your last display of humanity has left me more than a little uneasy," she replied. "What you offered was ridiculous. Three days to guess your name? Giving that blasted quill to Edward instead of me? You wanted his signature instead of mine, even though the debt was not his to pay. I want to know why."

"Always so suspicious! Can't I just be generous?" I snapped. "I gave you a chance. True, I might have placed the responsibility of this new contract on your dear husband, but I thought it time he protect someone other than himself for once. I don't see what you are so concerned about. I've granted your every request, and yet you still don't seem to trust me."

"Why should I?" she asked with a delicately-arched scornful eyebrow.

"Let me ask you. Have you gotten everything you wanted so far? Haven't I always been true to my word?"

She was silent for a moment, but in the end remained unmoved. "None of that matters."

"How so?" I asked, surprised.

"Because I know you hate him. You hate him more than I do. I see it smoldering behind your eyes. Even now it burns," she said, taking slow, deliberate steps towards me. "I can't trust anything you do when it is all born out of a hatred such as yours."

I swiftly moved back to keep the distance between us.

"I told you that's my business," I warned.

"Not anymore," she said calmly, approaching close once more. "The moment you had me sign that first contract, your rage became *my* business. Tell me. What are you planning?"

I opened my mouth to tell her off, but no words came to me. No one had ever demanded an accounting of my motives. No one had ever dared to question me. No one...until a miller's daughter who became a queen and then a mother, and who now stood before me like a magnificent avenging goddess swathed in purple and gold.

"What did Edward do to you?" she pressed again, now standing toe-to-toe with me. "You want to break him, and I demand you tell me why!"

The perfume of her hair maddened me, and every dip and curve of her face begged for my kisses. There was no earthly reason I should desire her, should feel this agonizing yearning within my being to hold her and protect her from everything and everyone, including myself.

"You are just a coward, rigging a fight so no one but you has a chance of winning," she continued. "That's it, isn't it? You're just pulling the wings off a fly, the legs from a spider, and enjoying watching as it squirms."

I made no conscious decision. It was simply that one moment, she was standing there, berating me, and the next, I had grabbed her and pulled her against me, as if I could force my pain into her just by touching her. She had to understand. I had to make her understand. The black bile of my hate pushed up out of my throat, boiling over like lava, and there was no stopping the damage it was determined to cause.

"He destroyed everything in my life that I held dear," I snarled, pushing her toward the wall with my body. "I am only repaying the favor."

"Repaying the favor?" she laughed. "I'm just supposed to accept that as a reason for you to destroy everything I hold dear in my life? This is madness!"

"It is justice."

"There is no justice when innocents are sacrificed!"

I pushed until she was against the wall, with no place for her gaze to rest except upon me. Still, there was no fear in her, no sign of the terror she should have felt at my power or at the knowledge of my pain.

"Is that so?" I asked, not recognizing my own voice anymore. I was no longer in that room. I was no longer talking to Laila. I was lost to my rage. "Let me tell you about the sacrifice of innocents. Imagine your mother, your sweet mother, locked in a room. Trapped. Fire blazes all around you and you have to listen as she cries out for you to save her. You can smell her flesh burn, and there's nothing you can do but listen to her screams grow louder, more desperate, as flames broil her skin and singe her hair."

At last, I saw reaction in Laila. She tried to turn her face away, but I grabbed her chin, digging my fingers into her flesh and forcing her to look at me. She wanted to know the reason, so I would damn well make sure she knew everything.

"There are also a child's shrieks clawing at your brain. She is your sister. She is burning, and as her cries for mercy grow silent, you know it is because the flames have finally scorched her lungs."

Laila shook her head against my hold on her jaw, but I would not let her go. She thought she had felt trapped in that dungeon? Let her feel the horror of being truly trapped through my words.

"Don't forget your father, your loving father. You have to watch as the monarch he serves plunges a dagger into his chest. The sound of the metal scraping against his bones is the worst of all. *Snap. Pop.* Until there is a nauseous gurgle as blade meets heart and muscle."

I struck the wall with my hand, and a thunderous crack fueled by my magic and rage echoed darkly through the thousand fissures that chased along the stones down to the very foundations of the castle. A wave of pain rippled through my tendons but it was nothing against the agony of the memories that tore at my soul. She jumped in surprise as the stone rumbled behind her head. Pure horror shone from her eyes.

My throat was so tight I couldn't breathe as I released her and turned away. I couldn't look at her anymore. Retreating back to the hearth, I fell into a chair and leaned forward, pressing my elbows into my knees and resting my face in my hands. Silence loomed over us, heavy and wicked.

"I'm…sorry," she finally whispered.

"*Sorry?*" I repeated with disgust, not bothering to look up at her. "That won't fix much. I can still hear them screaming, you know. Still see the blood running out of my father's mouth and chest. I have been taunted, kicked, chased out and betrayed. I am haunted, Laila, and the ghosts will not leave me until the king's heart is silenced by my hand."

She swallowed hard and stared at me. I watched dully as she struggled to collect herself and summon some reserve of inner fortitude.

"And after the ghosts are gone," she asked. "What happens then?"

"That would ruin the surprise if I told you, and I'd hate for that to happen." I tried to sound bored and blasé, but I was too hollow to hold any malicious mirth. This was not exactly the way my revenge was supposed to play out. "Stop wasting my time with these questions and get to the real point. I know you didn't summon me here tonight just to offer your heartfelt condolences on the passing of my family. You want something more from me. I can smell it rising from your skin."

She took a deep breath and asked, "If Edward fails to discover your name, what do you intend to do with my son?"

"There is no need to concern yourself. The child will be well protected, remember? You weaseled your way into getting me to sign my name to shelter it from any and all danger. I couldn't let harm befall him even if I wanted to. Isn't that knowledge enough to let you sleep at night? Isn't that what you wanted? For you to be free of the screaming and the wailing of those infernal little lungs while you enjoyed being queen?"

She let her gaze fall to the floor. "I thought that's what I wanted," she confessed. "I was wrong. I see that now. A child needs a parent's love. Otherwise, you are nothing but lost and scared. An orphan forever wondering why you were abandoned. I don't want that fate for Tristan. I love him. I love him with my entire being and I want him to know my love. Don't you see?"

I didn't answer.

"Kill Edward," she spat. "Take his kingdom and land. Take my wealth and title. I'd give it all up to stay with my child...to love him and be with him always. That is what I want. My debt cleared so my child can have its mother. Perhaps then I can start repenting for my sins. You know what it is like to grow up without a mother. Would you condemn another to your fate?"

I laughed at her. Cold poison coursed through my veins now, and it killed any remorse she hoped to spark. If only I wanted the king's blood. I wanted his suffering, and that child was the only way.

"Can you really clear a debt such as yours?" I asked. "A mother who signed away their child, bound it to me with their own blood? You are truly stupid to think it could be such a simple thing to change. It is forever. Eternal. You belong to me, *miller's daughter*, since the moment your father took my bait."

An icy chill overcame her features.

"What are you saying?" she asked.

"Does this really surprise you that much? You really don't know how deep this all goes. How do you think the king discovered your little talent? Why would your father claim you could do something I just happen to be rather skilled at doing?"

She paled, and her pupils widened with shock.

"That's right. I was there, whispering in his ear, egging your father on. How lucky that night there happened to be a group of guards to overhear him. He was happy to spin his tales in exchange for the river of whiskey I bought him."

"You are a monster," she said in a tone of quiet, horrified wonder, as if finally realizing the truth of the matter.

"I'm far worse," I replied darkly. I could no longer bear her looks of both compassion and revulsion. I told myself it was because I had had my fill of her whining. I stood and turned away, preparing to vanish to anywhere but there.

"Edward will find your name," she said softly, moving to stand over the crib where her infant son slept. "I will keep my son. And you? You will have to live knowing you have become the very thing you hate."

The miller's daughter spoke as if she conjured both prophesy and curse. My blood ran cold. I thought of summoning my magic and vanishing, but I couldn't escape the feeling that something had just gone terribly, dangerously wrong.

UNHAPPILY: LAILA

I **picked up** Tristan, careful of his precious, sleepy form. He was still so tiny, impossibly tiny yet perfect with all those toes and fingers. He was the one gift Edward had ever given me that I was truly grateful for, and I did not hate the part of Edward that was him.

The stranger sat silently next to the fire, his thoughts lost in its flames. I shuddered at his revelations and felt an unwelcome wave of compassion for him. I couldn't help but trace the lines of rage and grief reflected in the elegant lines of his brooding, handsome face. Oh, what a farce my life had become! Fascinated by a stranger while I held my son by another man. I disgusted myself. Yet, if there was one thing that could redeem me, it would be to save my son.

Desperation and pain once again made me clever.

"What if I came with you?" I asked quietly.

The stranger looked up sharply, narrowing his eyes at me.

"There is nothing in the contract that says that I may not accompany my son when he passes into your possession," I persisted gently, allowing the faintest trickles of hope and humility through the sluice gate of my emotions. "You do not want the care of this child, and by bringing me with you, your vow to see the child well cared-for would be fulfilled."

The stranger raised his brows mockingly, but I could tell by the twist of his mouth that he was actually considering my offer. I turned more fully toward him, letting my breasts rise and fall with my breath. His eyes grew dark as he understood my other, silent offer. I gave him nothing but honesty with my eyes. I knew deep within my secret self that I would gladly give my body to him, but in that moment, I realized that I would also give him my love, and a lifetime of patience to heal his heart. I shook from the enormity of it all.

He opened his mouth to speak, and the door to the room flew open, banging against the wall as Edward strode in, grinning like a cat with the cream.

"You needn't hunch over the babe like a she-wolf," he proclaimed. "We have nothing to fear from that man. He's a coward."

"Is that so?" the stranger said coldly, suddenly standing behind Edward. "What a rude thing to say. But then, you never were one much for manners."

"I was wondering when you would grace us with your presence. I was beginning to think you'd gotten lost," Edward said with a self-satisfied smile. "Care for some wine?"

The man curled his lips in disgust, and his eyes darkened with rage. I could barely breathe from fear.

"I haven't come here to drink your rotgut," he hissed. "I've come for something far more precious. Your child. Now, if you would kindly hand him over, I would love to be on my way. Don't want to make this messier than it already is."

He walked towards me, and I tightened my grip on Tristan. Edward put out his arm, preventing the stranger from coming any closer. For the first time, I was grateful for his foolish bravery. The stranger only gave an annoyed smirk.

"Problem?" he asked.

"Yes, actually," Edward replied. "You told me I had three days to guess your name. Don't you want to know if I succeeded?"

Rumpelstiltskin's body stiffened, but he nodded in acceptance.

"Be my guest. Let's see what that fine mind of yours was able to concoct."

He went back to the chair and sat down, pressing his fingertips together in an exquisitely sarcastic steeple.

Edward clapped his hands, and in rushed a servant holding a long scroll. The king took it from him and slowly unrolled the parchment, revealing it to be filled with names. Hundreds of names.

The man pressed his fingers harder together and I could briefly see his jaw clench behind them.

"Since you last saw us, I've made it my mission to discover every name in the kingdom. Collecting them as you can plainly see on this scroll, here." He patted the paper. "Let's see which is yours."

Confusion overcame me momentarily for the reason for such theatrics until I realized the objective. Edward was playing a game, as he always did. He wanted to watch the stranger squirm, just as he watched me squirm when he threw me in that dungeon of straw. Only once his prey's anxiety reached the level he desired would he go in for the kill.

A vicious smile pulled on Edward's lips as he began the hunt.

"Is your name William?" he asked.

The man shook his head and cleared his throat.

"What about Thomas?"

"No," he replied firmly.

"Gerhardt, perhaps?"

It went on like this for several minutes, and with each passing name, the man relaxed. He let his hands fall to his lap and crossed his knee. That familiar nonchalance he loved to exhibit returned full force.

"Yuri?"

"Come, you must do better than that."

"Klaus?"

"God in heavens no!"

"Well, it has to be Victor."

The man laughed and stood from his chair, but his laugh didn't ring true. It didn't' hold the easy triumph that it usually did. There was a sharp, dangerous metallic sound to it now, and I feared the worst.

"Are we quite finished with this rubbish?" he asked Edward. "Obviously you don't know anything about who I am. I can't stand here all night while you waste my time with a bunch of nonsense. Now, if you'll kindly excuse me, I am going to take what's rightfully mine."

"Just one moment," Edward said in a jovial tone. "How about one more?"

"Do you really think that will do you much better than what you've already tried?" he asked. "Or does that thick skull of yours not know when to call it quits?"

"Oblige me."

The stranger eyed Edward, wary at the new, calm, cool tone in his voice. "Fine. One more and then you are through."

Edward gave a devilish smile as he threw the scroll to the floor. He was ready for his kill. He approached him with narrowed eyes and proceeded to inspect him up and down.

"Since I have only one guess left. Let's make it a good one, shall we? Something rare. Something that I wouldn't have thought about in twenty-eight years." He leaned in and whispered, "Something like...*Rumpelstiltskin*."

Deadly silence followed.

"Who told you that?" he growled.

CHAPTER TWELVE

UNHAPPILY: RUMPELSTILTSKIN

Hatred burned in my stomach, and my hands shook as everything I wanted crumbled with a word. I truly was a fool to have ever offered him such a deal.

"Who the devil told you that name?" I demanded again.

Rage boiled in my heart, flooding my skin with heat. I wanted nothing more than to sink my fingers into the king's face and rip that smug look from his skull.

"I can hardly recognize you," the king continued as he inspected me closer. "You look nothing like your father. He was a warrior. You... you look like a weakling. Perhaps your mother dallied with a footman, and your father was too kind-hearted to disown you."

"You're the only bastard here," I snapped.

"Is that any way to address your king? You have no right to speak to me that way. In fact, you have no rights whatsoever. All you have is a wicked tongue and some parlor tricks. Other than that, you are nothing but an ingrate. A worm I intend to squash beneath my boot."

"You'd better be very careful or—"

"Or what?" the king taunted. "What on earth are you going to do? You've lost, and my son remains mine. The crown is once again secured from those freakish fingers of yours."

He signaled to his guards and they quickly approached with drawn swords. There were more of them than last time, but I wasn't concerned. My mind was too busy racing through a thousand possibilities to find the one way of turning all this to my advantage once again.

"Now I am going to finish what I should have all those years ago and reunite you with your dearly departed family. Be sure to say hello to your mother for me. She was a pretty thing, if I remember rightly."

"If you think you can kill me, then you are stupider than I thought," I said, fighting to regain control of myself and the situation. "You might have found my name and remembered the boy I was, but that doesn't mean I still can't kill you."

His smile vanished, replaced by pure annoyance. The guards charged, but with one twist of my hand, a chorus of snapping necks echoed through the room. Their bodies fell like limp rags onto the floor, and a helmet rolled to a stop at my feet.

"I've waited too long for this moment," I said. "You have no idea how much I've dreamt about this day. It was going to be slow, agonizing. I was going to enjoy your misery, to age it like a fine wine in oak."

"I suppose now you are just going to snap my neck like you did these guards instead?" Edward asked, drawing his sword. "Then you would be a coward."

"No, I would be infinitely smarter than what I plan to do," I replied, conjuring a sword in my hand. "But, at the very least, I intend to serve you out the way you did my father. While lacking true artistry, it will at least be a magnificent gesture of justice."

We circled one another. The rush of feet and silk skirts ran past me as Laila tried for the door. I stopped her in her tracks with a wave of my hand, immobilizing her and the child in her arms completely. She couldn't miss the show. Not after how hard I worked for it.

Taking this as an opportune moment, the king struck with his sword. Clashing metal echoed through the room as I quickly blocked his blow.

"You amaze me," he said as he swung at me again. "You wait all these years plotting and planning, coming up with some intricate game only to get this far and fail, for you will fail."

I lunged at him and our blades crossed again. The sound of steel etching across steel pained my ears. He knocked me back and flung a chair in my path, but I kicked it out of the way. The wood splintered as it hit the wall. If only it had been his face.

We came at each other once more, our swords striking together in a symphony of clangs and scrapes.

"Why do you think I've failed?" I asked, backing him up against the table. Goblets of wine and dishes of rich foods spilled to the floor.

"Have you not?" he replied, striking out with his free hand, his fist crashing into my nose and sending me stumbling back. Pain spread through my brain like branches of lightning. "You wanted to steal my heir and take my throne. That's always been your plot. The same plot as your father. You are both the same vile creature. Although, I'd venture to say you have outdone him, becoming some sort of monster straight from hell."

My head still throbbing, I grunted with rage and swung my sword blindly. I felt a raw satisfaction as I saw the point slice into his cheek and blood drip down in long, red streaks. He groaned in agony like a wounded dog.

"I'm the monster?" I asked, taking my chance to close in on him. "You're the one that delights in terror and torture. Look what you did to Laila, threatening her life with an impossible task, just for a bit of sport. You're barbaric."

"Why do you care what I did to her?" he asked, licking the blood from his lips. He narrowed his eyes, and a malicious grin split his face. "You're in love with her! Ha, ha! That is the best joke! Fate must truly have a wicked sense of humor to curse you thus!"

I hit him as hard as I could with my sword, as if to knock away the awful sudden truth of his words, but he blocked my blow and held firm. Our blades shook as they slid downwards, and we glared murderously at each other.

"You're wrong," I said through clenched teeth. "I only care about one thing."

"What is that?"

"Your death."

"Then this will be a great disappointment for you."

There was a quick, burning, agonizing sensation between my ribs. I gasped for air, but my lungs struggled to fill. I watched smug gratification wash over the king's face. He thrust me back, and I stumbled, grabbing at the wall for support. I looked down to see a small dagger lodged deep in my chest.

"Funny," he said. "That I should kill both father and son with the same blade. One might even call it poetic justice."

I pulled the dagger out, wincing, but already, my body was healing itself. The magic I had been given by Fate had kept me alive through far worse than this. It was my turn for gratification as I saw the king's smirk fade and be replaced with doubt and then fear.

"Poetic indeed," I said, gazing at the blade.

Before he could move, I lunged at him and sunk his dagger deep into his chest, knowing I had hit his heart when the tip of the blade met resistance.

"You lose," I whispered in his ear.

An intense thrill flowed through me as I twisted the blade. Blood seeped from his mouth and nose, while his eyes grew hollow. I let him drop to the floor with the weight of my vengeance that was no more.

It was done.

I waited for the triumph to fill me.

I remained empty. Exhausted. Unable to care.

Glancing over at Laila and the baby, I absently flicked my fingers in their direction, removing the freezing spell. I turned back to contemplate the body of my enemy on the floor, barely hearing her gasp behind me.

"I've made you a widow," I said evenly.

She came to stand beside me, shielding the babe from the sight of its dead father.

"I can't pretend to mourn him," she said, though her bright eyes betrayed her. "He chose his path, just as you chose yours. If this is where it led him, so be it."

"Always so cold," I remarked sourly, unreasonable jealousy of her affection for a dead man running poisonously through my veins. "I sometimes wonder if that heart of yours is made completely of ice."

"It is not," she said. "It never was. I was desperate and in danger, and I made choices because of it. But, I was never without feeling."

She sighed, sounding as tired as I felt, and stroked the baby's downy hair. "It is over now, though. We are all free. We can begin again."

Dread seized my vitals and squeezed with bloody claws.

"No, we cannot," I said. "There is still your contract."

Laila stared at me, rage and horror dancing in her dark eyes.

"That's not possible!" she exclaimed. "Edward guessed your name. I heard him say it with my own ears. We know who you are, *Rumpelstiltskin*. We don't owe you our child anymore. The contract has been fulfilled."

My tongue felt leaden and reluctant in my mouth, but I forced it to form the words.

"Yes and no," I murmured. "His contract was fulfilled, but yours isn't."

"Explain," she demanded.

"You were right in not wanting him to sign the contract I gave him," I said with a sigh. "Very astute of you, really. Pity he didn't listen to your keen warnings. Sadly, he signed in his blood and now he is dead. That means the deal I offered him was rendered null and void the moment that vicious heart of his rung out its last infernal beat. However, as the blood was not your own, your deal with me still stands firm. That is why you have lost your child."

"A loophole," she said through clenched teeth. "I knew you'd do something like this."

I gritted my teeth against a sudden wave of shame and guilt that I didn't want to feel, for they were too closely connected to a truth I wanted to deny with all my heart: that I loved Laila.

"Of course I did something like this," I snapped. "I built in loopholes to the loopholes in the contracts. I was not prepared to sacrifice my vengeance for anyone, nor would I risk it with any chance."

"Now you have your vengeance! Edward is dead and everything he had is yours. Why do you still demand my child? Just let us go. Break the contract!" she cried.

I sighed. If only things would be so simple.

"You don't understand. I can't break it," I said, glancing at the child. "The magic running through the page is bound to your blood. It is insoluble. The only way to be released from the contract is to go through with it."

"I don't believe you," she shrieked, tears running down her face. "You can break it. You just don't want to. You want everyone to suffer just like you. To feel the misery you damned yourself to wallow in."

Her tears nearly undid me, but they could not undo the contract. Her accusations cut me deeper than any dagger ever could, and there was no magic to heal the heartache they left behind. She thought so little of me, she disdained me! She would be glad to be rid of me, and yet, I would never be complete again without her fire. Pain reared in my heart, fueling a fiery rage.

"You are never satisfied!" I shot back. "You know nothing! You do nothing—except take and take. Maybe it is *you* who are the true monster here!"

Her eyes widened, and I swallowed down my hurt. I couldn't get into all this. Not now, not when the magic of the contract was beginning to pull at me, tugging raggedly at the edges of my magic.

"Give me the child," I said. "Trust me and do as I say. You cannot break the contract. The child will be safe. I am bound to this just as much as you."

The contract appeared in my hand, demanding its payment. That flame of desperation blazed in her chest as her eyes locked on the roll of paper in my grip.

She came to me, and I held my breath, waiting for her to hand me the child. She snatched the contract out of my hand and cast it into the fire.

Green sparks rose up from the flames, and the paper itself seemed to moan as it was consumed.

"What have you done?" I cried, aghast. "You little fool! There are more things at play here than just you and me. Damn you!"

Laila jumped back, her face filled with alarm as she clutched the babe fiercely to her breast. Frantically, I tried to think of what kind of magic would hold back what was coming, or whether I could write a new contract in the seconds that remained.

The walls and floors began to quake, pebbles and dust raining down on us.

It was too late. I was too late.

A vortex of utter darkness opened in the ceiling and swirled violently above us. I leapt over to Laila and pulled us to the ground, shielding her with my body. She held onto my shoulder with her free hand, looking up into my eyes with utter despair and an emotion I could not name. I ran my fingers through her hair, letting my thumb caress her cheek, uncaring that tears ran down my own.

Too late. Too late!

Three dark figures stretched unnaturally down from the vortex, their red eyes glowing as they flexed their long, dead fingers.

"What are they?" Laila whispered raggedly, huddling into my protective embrace.

"The Furies," I choked out. "They come for those who—"

"Oath breaker!" they screamed, rushing at Laila.

I sent a blast of magic at them, but they dove right through it, unfazed. A flick of their fingers, and I was on my back, pinned to the floor, unable to do anything but watch in horror as they grabbed Laila by her arms and hair, dragging her toward the vortex.

I summoned every ounce of power I possessed and broke free of their spell, lunging forward and grabbing Laila by the wrist. I rooted my magic down through the floors, into the earth itself. I sent blast after blast of raw power at the creatures.

"Please!" Laila begged between gasps and screams as they dug their claws into her flesh. "Please!"

I knew what she was trying to say. It was the same thing the compulsion that now sang in my blood demanded.

Let her go.

Save the child.

The contract was calling on my blood, demanding I meet the terms. I braced every nerve and sinew in my body to resist, but the oath magic was inexorable.

"Don't tell him what I did," she sobbed. "Don't ever let him know the shame of his mother. If there is only one kindness you ever show me, let it be this."

She released the baby just as I was compelled to release her wrist and catch him. Laila flew deep into the embrace of the monsters, who retreated into the darkness, pulling it up behind them.

There was nothing left. Only silence, the crackling of the fire, and a dead king on the floor.

Laila's son wailed in my arms, demanding my attention be on it alone. I looked down at him. Though he had his father's eyes, the rest of his features were undeniably his mother's. Bitterly, I realized I would never be free of either of them now that I was bound to their babe.

I wanted to yell at Tristan to quit his squalling, but all I could do was coo and murmur gently in defiance of my heart, "Hush, it's all right now. You're safe."

A tear I didn't realize I had shed fell onto his smooth cheek, and I brushed it away.

"What drama! What tragedy!" someone exclaimed sardonically behind me, clapping his hands. "A shame it all had to make such an awful mess. The inlay on the floor will never quite be the same, but that is unfortunately how these things usually end."

I turned around and was met by the angelic face and striking blue eyes of Fate. He looked just as he did the last time I saw him.

"A shame she didn't believe you," he said. "You could have returned the child to her once the goods were exchanged. Ohhhh, by the look on your face, I can see you didn't think of that. Or, perhaps you didn't know that such a thing was possible with those kinds of oaths. Well, perhaps it's as good a time as any for you to remember that *anything* can be negotiated in this life."

With perfect, icy, calmness, I walked back to the crib and gently placed Tristan down among the covers, carefully drawing the blanket over him. I then walked back to Fate, ready to use all of my power to blast him back to the shades of Hell.

"You may be asking yourself what I'm doing here," he quipped, seeming not at all bothered by my menace. "I came to offer you my congratulations! It's not every day I witness such a beautifully gruesome end of a mortal. You did very well, just as I hoped."

He strode over to the king's body and nudged it delicately with the toe of his boot.

"I'm glad I lived up to your standards," I ground out between my teeth, holding my magic in abeyance by some warning instinct.

"Of course," he said, "you don't deserve all the credit. I might have helped just a tiny bit. I can't help myself from meddling. It's in my nature, you know."

"What do you mean by *helped?*" I demanded, suspicions too dreadful to name rolling relentlessly through my mind.

He smiled and knelt down next to the king's corpse. He took off the heavy crown and examined the shimmering jewels set deep within the gold.

"For starters, let's just say the king certainly enjoyed my little ditty when he came romping through the woods last night. He was awfully curious of what I had to tell him. Poor fellow! You didn't set him a very easy task having to guess your name."

Acid burned in my breast. I felt sick. He stood up and tossed the crown to the floor where it landed with a heavy clatter.

"You're the one that told him?" I panted. "You're who robbed me of what I was promised?"

He placed a firm finger against my lips. "I promised you nothing. I simply gave you what you required to do the job."

I slapped his hand away. He looked pleased, ecstatic even.

"You told me death was too quick, that I should savor his demise," I reminded him. "Why would you take that away from me?"

"It's true that I did say that, but I grew impatient with your rather complicated schemes. I decided a quick and clean solution was far better to get you to where I truly want you," he said.

"Where you truly want me? And just where is that?"

"You keep seeming to forget who you are dealing with," he said, suddenly sharp. "I'm not some guardian angel sent to help you along life's journey. I'm Fate. I push and I prod, inching you along to where I desire you to be. I've always been interested in you, Rumpelstiltskin. From the moment you were born, I knew I wanted you."

He cupped my cheek in his hand and laughed wickedly. My throat ran dry. He caressed my skin with his thumb, and I knew I was nothing more than his slave, his puppet. I had been doing his bidding since the moment I took my first breath. I snapped my head away from his touch and grabbed my but the collar of his shirt.

"What all have you done?" I seethed, shaking him.

He seemed to delight in my rage, and his eyes glowed even brighter. "Just a nudge here and there. Very much like what you've accomplished with your own little game. Do you really think you'd be where you are right now if it wasn't for me?"

The knuckles of my fists grew white.

"I was the one who planted the seed of fear of treason from your father in Edward's troubled mind. I was the one who pushed him to thin the bloodline to the throne, eliminating family after family. I was the guard who pulled you from the flames and told you to run, and how fast and far your feet carried you! Right back into my welcoming arms."

The blue-eyed soldier floated through my memory.

"That was you?" I cried.

"Honestly, you think these things just *happen?* If I hadn't been there to secure the destiny awaiting you, all your potential would've been unforgivably wasted. Can you imagine? You'd still be stuck in that large house filled with unending family squabbles, condemned to live as a mediocre squire to thankless peasants and a fool for a king. You should thank me for saving you from such a horrendously dull life, really. What I have in store for you will be far more rewarding."

Rage blazing through my veins, I lifted him up and slammed him into the wall. The room trembled.

"Then my fight has been with the wrong person," I spat. "My God! You've been manipulating me this entire time!"

He grinned, looking untroubled by any pain, even as spidery cracks spread behind his head. "A person consumed by their past is always easy to manipulate because they have no thought for the future. Besides, there really is no one to be upset with but yourself. Yes, I might have interfered, but I don't deserve all the blame. I can't make you do anything you do not choose yourself. That is the unfortunate limit of my powers."

A grimace befell his features and he looked regretful, as if remembering something he wanted to forget. However, he quickly caught himself and hid it away.

"I can only present a map of paths, Rumpelstiltskin. It was you who chose the ones you took. You chose to accept the magic I offered and you chose a life dedicated to pain. Free will has been your enemy, not me."

"I swear I will never rest until this world is rid of you!" I bellowed, shoving him again. His head cracked against the wall hard enough to kill a man, but he only laughed.

"Such spark! You don't know how long I've waited for someone like you!" he chuckled. "It's too bad that you can't destroy me. It's ironic really, that Fate has no fate. I have no end. I cannot be stopped. It is too late, Rumpelstiltskin. You can try and escape your destiny, but your choices will always mark you."

Scorching pain flared in my hand, searing my flesh to the bone. I cried out, dropping him instantly. I gazed at the scar on my palm, the wicked reminder of the well of power he had poured into me. I braced myself against the agonizing pain, unwilling to let a single sound escape me, as the scar stretched and grew, snaking along the other lines of my hand until every path upon my palm was marked.

My shackling was complete.

His shadow loomed over me.

"I am looking forward to what I have in store for you," Fate said, his voice less amused and darker than I had ever heard it. "I'm positive you will make it a work of art."

With that, he vanished, leaving me raw, deceived, and shamed on the floor.

I stared at the map of scars on my hand, his words burning in my mind between flashes of Laila's face as the Furies took her.

He had said free will was my enemy? He would soon learn it would be his.

I had no more free will, no more choice. There was only one place my path would lead me now.

To his grave.

EXCERPT FROM "TWIST: A FAIRY TALE AWAKENING," BOOK TWO

Nineteen Years Later

Rumpelstiltskin

"**You think you're** being followed?"

"That's the point, I don't know," I said. "I don't know if I'm being followed, wanted, or hunted. There is only the sensation. This dark energy leering over my shoulder. I've ignored every chill rippling down my back, until now."

I scrubbed my face with my hand. I wasn't used to experiencing such a lack of knowledge. Control. It terrified me.

"Why until now?" Aldred asked.

I pulled out a deck of tarot cards from my inner pocket. Their edges were frayed and corners bent with age. I laid them out across the table of gnarled oak.

One, two horizontal across the first, three moving counter clock-wise to four, five, six. To the right of the cross I placed a card at the bottom and placed three more one above the other—seven, eight, nine, ten.

Aldred stroked his beard, his thick silver rings fresh against his leathered skin.

The edges pressed into my thumb as I slid and flipped them over. Blood thrashed in my ears as I saw again what I loathed to see.

"What do you make of it?" I asked.

He leaned closer in, his eyes scanning the garden of wands, cups, and swords. The wrinkles on Aldred's ancient face deepened with concern.

"Gibberish."

"Precisely," I said. "I've laid out these cards one hundred and two times and each time it is the same. Unreadable. Suns and towers. Hearts and ten of swords. I've been cut off from my own future. I rely on knowing as much as possible, especially with this spectral chill. This feeling does not come without purpose and the cards do not stop revealing without intervention."

It is too late, Rumpelstiltskin. You can try and escape your destiny, but your choices will always mark you, Fate's voice resonated in my memory.

The scar he had left me burned across my palm.

Tarot cards, crystal gazing, tea leaves, any form of divination were my only weapon against Fate. How I deprived him of entwining me further in whatever sick scheme he wanted. They allowed me to plan. Plot. Map out which steps to take and which to avoid. No choice would come unstudied again. Now, my path was gone. My neat and tidy bricks were left trailing into nothing but mist.

Fear cut through my core again like a blade of ice.

"This is why you sought me out," Aldred said.

"I had nowhere else to turn," I replied.

Aldred, the scholar. Educated by the finest universities and expert in the black arts. Though he was not an immortal being as I was, no one knew more about the craft.

"If you are being followed or hunted, what, or who, do you think it is?"

I am looking forward to what I have in store for you, Fate's voice echoed again.

I clenched my jaw. Blood rushed through my heart and terror chilled my veins. I hated this feeling of vulnerability. In my heart I wished it were the devil, or some other manner of dark creature, but I knew only one being would toy with me like this.

I only hoped what I suspected was wrong.

"Only you know of what happened all those years ago," I said.

"You mean with the girl..."

I bit the inside of my lip, Laila's memory still raw in my gut after all these years.

"I allowed myself to become such a fool at Fate's hands. I can't have it happen again. I've taken every precaution to rid myself of such an error," I said.

"You believe Fate is preparing to use you to fulfill some destiny?"

I remained silent. Such a thought was abhorrent to me, but it was what I feared. And now without being able to see my future...

He cleared his throat.

"Does the boy know?"

"No." I paced across the groaning floorboards, careful to avoid his towers of books. "I swore to his mother never to tell him the truth of what happened between her and I. It's one of the reasons he despises me."

He gave a pitying look.

"I'm sure it's not come to that. You've raised him well all these years. The heart remembers what good has been done towards it."

I wasn't sure. As Tristan grew so did my guilt, and a distance took root between us. I couldn't help but associate Tristan with loss.

I recalled how I started to crave the distance. The numbness. I journeyed farther and longer away, hunting desperate souls that would help soothe my own.

"I can bear his scorn for Laila," I said.

He rested his hand on my shoulder.

"Perhaps this sensation is not Fate, but only a manifestation of your guilt."

I chuckled.

"I've lived with my guilt so long I'm perfectly used to the sensation. No, this has Fate's stench all over it. But without the cards, I can't be certain."

I shook off his hand.

"I know what you are wanting. She is too dangerous," he said.

"I am well aware, but I have no choice. I must find her. My powers of foresight are not strong enough. Only she can tell me what I can do to avoid what I fear."

"I've seen men go mad from what she told them," he replied, urgency burning in every word. "I swore I would never tell another soul where she keeps. You must accept not knowing and adapt."

"It is not in my nature to adapt."

Anything that wasn't certain garnered my suspicion.

"Oracles are precarious creatures. Their riddles only promise further burden," he pleaded.

"That is a risk I will take. The boy is still in my care, I am bound by his mother to never allow him harm. If this is Fate moving pawns, then it won't only affect me, it might also hurt Tristan. I will not let that happen. I need her to see what these cards are preventing me from seeing," I said. "I need her to tell me what my future holds so I can avoid it."

He exhaled slowly, shaking his head.

"I'm sorry, but there are times it is best to leave what will be what will be," he said.

My stomach pitted. Aldred possessed a fierce stubborn streak. It is what I respected and detested about him.

"You refuse?"

"You must view this as an opportunity."

Opportunity? I hated that word. I clenched my fingers into fists as heat flushed over my skin.

"I'm still a dangerous man," I said.

He stiffened.

"I know," he replied.

"Then you should also know I don't want to hurt you, but if you remain standing in the way of what I want, you leave me no choice."

"I do not fear death."

I grimaced. His mind was too logical to dread the unknown.

"Men wise as you rarely do, which is why it pains me to do this..."

A simple twist of my wrist filled the room with his screams. Pressing his hands against his skull he tried to stop the obvious pain pounding within his brain. His face twisted and his breaths grew short.

I twisted my wrist again. I closed my eyes, but I wished I could have silenced my ears. I hated this part of me capable of such torture.

Another scream.

"I can make it stop if you tell me what I want," I coaxed, hoping he would break and I could end his torment.

I opened my eyes. He slid down the wall, his fingers white from the pressure as he continued to push against his temples. His red eyes stared up at me, a beautiful flame of desperation igniting within his soul telling me all I needed to know.

He was ready.

I released my hold on him. He gasped several large breaths and leaned his head against the wall.

His fingers trembled as he pointed at a bookcase, its shelves bending from the weight of heaped books and strewn parchment. I roved across the peeling bindings until I saw what I desired.

Wedged between the chaos was an unassuming box of gray lead. Ugly thing, yet inside—absolute beauty.

A disc of gold. No. Rings of gold, I should say. Six of them in all, each fitting tightly within the other. I took it out and laid it in my palm. I'd read of its ability. Its power. But it was another thing entirely to see it. To hold such a priceless object in my hand.

I waved over it. The bands whistled and hummed as they opened like flower petals. The bands crisscrossed, forming a perfect armillary sphere.

"She...she..." Aldred gasped between large gulps of air. "She exiled herself to the Forest of Enduring Shadows. It is endless. One could spend centuries searching its vastness. The only way to find her is to use the Sphere of Asteria. She is bound to its magic. She feared the destruction her knowledge caused humanity, what men did with her prophecies. She hid herself away to stop the torment."

I waved my hand over the sphere again and the bands fell flat into a disc. I stuffed it into my satchel.

"I take no pleasure in hurting you," I said.

He nodded.

"Rumpelstiltskin," he said. "It is sometimes best to accept what will be. You've run from destiny so long..."

I looked down at the cards that showed senseless nothings. I wondered for a heartbeat what it would be like to continue not knowing. To push forward into the mist of the future.

The hair on my neck prickled and the fear returned. The scar on my hand burned. I believed myself drowning in an ocean.

I gathered my cards and put them back into my pocket.

"I do not run from destiny. I make my own."

THANK YOU!

I sincerely hope you enjoyed reading this book as much as I enjoyed writing it. If you did, I would greatly appreciate a short review on Amazon or your favorite book website, such as Goodreads! Reviews are crucial for any author, and even just a line or two can make a huge difference.

ALSO BY GENEVIEVE RAAS

NOVELS

The ***Spindlewind Trilogy***, a dark fantasy, paranormal romance retelling of Rumpelstiltskin

Spin

Twist

Break

NOVELLAS

Crimp

A gothic romance. Enjoy as a stand alone work, or as a companion to the *Spindlewind Trilogy*.

The Crown

A dark retelling of the *Twelve Dancing Princesses*

ALSO BY RAVENWELL PRESS

The *Spirit Seeker Series*, a YA, epic fantasy adventure by
Award Winning Author Hannah Stahlhut

Wanderling

Resistance

Voyage

ACKNOWLEDGMENTS

I cannot express my thanks and gratitude enough to everyone who has helped me shape *Spin* into what you read today. They cheered me on and dried my tears. Most importantly, they never let me quit.

The person I have to thank first is the person who read it first. Hannah Stahlhut, you are a trooper! You not only read the never ending drafts, but did so willingly and with excitement. I don't know where I'd be without your feedback and advice. If that wasn't enough, in my panicked moments you were always willing to talk me through, and help me come up with a plan. For all this and so much more, I thank you.

Behind every writer is an editor. Cait Reynolds, you are simply unsurpassed! You saw within the rubble the gold shining through. Your knowledge and guidance helped transform *Spin* into what I envisioned. You pushed my limits, forced me away from my comfort zone, and made me a stronger writer for it. I hate to think where I would be if it weren't for you. You truly are my big sister and I love you. Thank you for more than you could know.

To my husband, Rafi, your continued encouragement and love throughout this lengthy project has always been my greatest strength. You were always willing to listen to me talk about my book, which was all the time. You rejoiced in my victories and lifted me up in my failures. In short, you kept me going. I love you with my entire being.

To my parents, you always believed and never blinked an eye when your daughter said she wanted to write a novel. Thank you for your love. Thank you for always being there and supporting me from the moment I first picked up a pencil and wrote little stories about foxes.

Thank you to Megan Linski, who also had a hand in editing *Spin*. You gave wonderful feedback, opinions, and suggestions that helped me make the changes I didn't want to admit.

A special thanks to Shari Ryan! She created a beautiful cover and is also to thanks for formatting *Spin* into its final product.

Finally, to my friend Michael, I wouldn't have written this book if you hadn't introduced me to what started it all. Thank you!

To all my other family and friends who gave me their continued support and excitement, simply, thank you. You were all insurmountable in keeping me strong and keeping me going.

ABOUT THE AUTHOR

Genevieve Raas is an international bestselling author living in the US with her husband and rather haughty Chihuahua, Mr. Darcy. When she isn't writing dark fairytales or fantasy, you can find her plotting out her next travel destination.

A graduate from Indiana University, Genevieve holds a Master's Degree in English and a Master's Certificate in Professional Editing. She has worked as Lead Transcriber on several published anthologies, including: The Collected Stories of Ray Bradbury, Volume 2 and the New Ray Bradbury Review.

Now, she is venturing out on her own, into the wilds of untamed lands and untold stories.

Genevieve writes gothic romance, dark fantasy, and horror.

Genevieve loves connecting with her readers!

www.genevieveraas.com

genevieveraas@genevieveraas.com

Made in the USA
Las Vegas, NV
09 December 2020

12389655R00122